23

THE VANQUISHERS

SECRET OF THE REAPING

BY KALYNN BAYRON

For younger readers

The Vanquishers
Secret of the Reaping

For older readers

Cinderella Is Dead
This Poison Heart
This Wicked Fate
You're Not Supposed to Die Tonight

THE VANQUISHERS

SECRET OF THE REAPING

KALYNN BAYRON

BLOOMSBURY
CHILDREN'S BOOKS
NEW YORK LONDON OXFORD NEW DELHI SYDNEY

BLOOMSBURY CHILDREN'S BOOKS
Bloomsbury Publishing Inc., part of Bloomsbury Publishing Plc
1385 Broadway, New York, NY 10018

BLOOMSBURY, BLOOMSBURY CHILDREN'S BOOKS,
and the Diana logo are trademarks of Bloomsbury Publishing Plc

First published in the United States of America in October 2023
by Bloomsbury Children's Books
www.bloomsbury.com

Bloomsbury books may be purchased for business or promotional use.
For information on bulk purchases please contact Macmillan Corporate and
Premium Sales Department at specialmarkets@macmillan.com

Library of Congress Cataloging-in-Publication Data
available upon request
ISBN 978-1-5476-1157-7 (hardcover) • ISBN 978-1-5476-1158-4 (e-book)

Book design by Jeanette Levy
Typeset by Westchester Publishing Services
Printed and bound in the U.S.A.
2 4 6 8 10 9 7 5 3 1

To find out more about our authors and books visit
www.bloomsbury.com and sign up for our newsletters.

Remember, vampires are confused by rhymes.
Recite one to keep the undead at bay.

THE VANQUISHERS

SECRET OF THE REAPING

CHAPTER 1

Mr. Rupert is our resident Vanquisher historian and vampire history expert. The big whiteboard in my basement is filled with his chicken-scratch handwriting. There are timelines and squiggly arrows pointing to clusters of indecipherable words. He's mad that me, Cedrick, and Jules keep asking him to just tell us what he wants us to know instead of writing it on the board but he doesn't listen.

"You know," Cedrick says, leaning back in his chair and running his hand over the top of his head. "We have to take penmanship in school. Like, we get graded on it and everything. Did you take penmanship classes, Mr. Rupert?"

I look down into my lap, letting my braids fall across my face like a curtain. Jules pushes their shoulder into mine as we try really hard not to laugh.

"Do you know how old I am?" Mr. Rupert asks. He scowls so hard the lines on his forehead turn into deep, angry creases. "Do you know how long it's been since I was in grade school?"

I just shake my head. Mr. Rupert should know by now not to ask questions like that around Cedrick. It's an invitation for a roasting of epic proportions. I glance at Ced and he's grinning so hard he looks like his teeth are about to break. He's gonna go straight for the jugular. I just know it.

"Ooooh! Let me guess!" Ced runs his hand over his chin like a movie villain, then narrows his eyes at Mr. Rupert. "I'm gonna say . . . seventy. You're seventy years old. How close am I?"

If looks could kill, Cedrick would be dead and buried. Mr. Rupert presses his lips into a tight line and leans across the desk.

"I am fifty-three," he says flatly.

"Dang!" Cedrick says without missing a beat. "I was way off. But maybe you look older than you are? You know what they say."

"No," Mr. Rupert says. "What do they say?"

"Problematic people age like spoiled milk." Cedrick says it like it's a scientific fact and not something he probably heard online somewhere.

"So now I'm problematic?" Mr. Rupert asks. His voice is too high and his bald head is too sweaty for this to continue.

I swallow a laugh and clear my throat. "Mr. Rupert, are we done for the day?"

Mr. Rupert glances at his watch, then back to me. "Why? You have somewhere to be?"

I'm watching the clock, counting down the minutes until Aaron can safely come out and Mr. Rupert knows this. Aaron's a new vamp and we've learned that our theory about him being sensitive to the sun because he's a fledgling was correct. Mr. Rupert told us during a lesson that older vamps can walk around for hours in the daytime. I hate to admit it, but as much as Mr. Rupert annoys me, his lessons have a lot of helpful information. This little piece about vamps in the daylight is scary but I also hope that means that at some point Aaron can join us in the daytime. For now, I have to wait for him to wake up and climb out of the makeshift crypt his mom had made for him under the shed in their backyard.

"Focus, Miss Wilson, and put your attention here." Mr. Rupert points to something he's written in the corner of the whiteboard. "Make sure you are prepared."

"Is that an algebra equation?" Cedrick asks. "I see numbers and letters. Mr. Rupert, I don't want to learn math in here. I already have enough of that at school."

Mr. Rupert sighs.

I squint to make out the writing in the corner. "Does that say 'quiz'?" I ask.

Jules sits up straight. "A quiz, Mr. Rupert? Really?"

"You serious?" Cedrick asks. He slouches down in his seat. "See, problematic."

Mr. Rupert rolls his eyes and strums his fingers across his desk.

"This is way too much like regular school," Cedrick says. "When are we gonna learn to throw a stake into a vampire's neck?"

Mr. Rupert rubs his temple like he can't believe what he's hearing. "The heart, Cedrick. The stake goes in the heart."

Cedrick doesn't want any part of Mr. Rupert's lessons about Vanquisher history and vampire lore. He wants to fistfight a vampire and it's honestly a little weird how eager he is to do that. The thought of being face-to-face with a vampire that isn't Aaron terrifies me. Not Ced. He's been hassling Mr. Rupert about teaching us some actual fighting skills but Mr. Rupert dismisses the suggestion every time.

"Question," Jules says. "My braces are silver. If I bite a vamp, will that kill them?" They click their teeth together, showing off their new black-and-purple rubber bands that connect to their shiny braces.

Mr. Rupert stands up and crosses his arms over his chest. "I wouldn't suggest it. Your braces are stainless steel, which is an alloy. It's mostly chromium and aluminum."

Jules looks disappointed. "That sucks."

"I find it comical that you think you could get close enough to a vamp to bite it without it biting you first," Mr. Rupert says.

"When something's funny, you're supposed to smile or laugh," Cedrick chimes in. "Just so you know."

Mr. Rupert's expression doesn't change at all. "Let's review for our quiz, shall we?" He shuffles some papers around on his desk. "The Reaping took place on April 28, 2002. The Vanquishers had hunted the undead to near extinction but the last hive had a foothold here in San Antonio. They were dug in, like ticks."

"Gross," I say.

"The last hive were chased from their hiding spot in the Natural Bridge Caverns just north of downtown San Antonio," Mr. Rupert says. "The Vanquishers pursued the hive into the city. The battle was fierce and the Vanquishers suffered heavy losses." Mr. Rupert clears his throat before continuing. "Dayside had already perished and as the final battle was fought, Nightside was killed in the Pearl district where the vampires made their last stand."

"You were there, too, right?" I ask. I'd never heard talk about him actually being there but if he'd been the official record keeper of the Vanquishers for as long as he says he has, he must have been involved.

"I was close by," he says. "I, of course, tried to do my part but as the three of you don't seem to understand, vampires are a formidable foe. They are ruthless. They don't hesitate to inflict pain and devastation everywhere they go. They have no regard for human life and they won't hesitate to end you and the people you love most." He's lost in his own thoughts for a second, then he takes three sheets of paper from his briefcase, and hands them to me, Ced, and Jules.

Cedrick groans and slumps down in his chair. "Really?"

"Really," Mr. Rupert says, furrowing his brow so hard I can barely see his eyes. "Flip the paper over when you're finished. Your time begins now."

I read over the first question.

In what year were the Vanquishers officially formed?

I pencil in the answer. 1850.

Mr. Rupert doesn't waste any time. From day one of what me, Ced, and Jules are calling Vanquisher training academy, Mr. Rupert gets right down to it. The history and origin of the vampires themselves is murky but the history of the Vanquishers isn't as hard to pick apart. Basic stuff we've learned in school doesn't compare to the level of detail Mr. Rupert goes into and sometimes it makes my brain hurt. I continue my quiz.

In what publication were the slayers who served as precursors to the Vanquishers mentioned publicly for the first time?

I have to think hard. Maybe I'd been passing notes to Jules when Mr. Rupert had gone over this part but the answer wriggles its way to the front of my mind.

Freedom's Journal said a group of masked slayers killed a hive of three vamps in 1827.

Cedrick nudges the leg of my chair with his foot. I glance over at him as Mr. Rupert turns his back to us. Ced tips up his paper so I can see the hideous little sketch he's made of Mr. Rupert with wings and little pointy teeth.

Mr. Rupert suddenly spins around and snatches the paper from Cedrick's hand. He glares down at the sketch and when he returns his gaze to Cedrick, his eyes are narrow and angry.

"How dare you depict me as one of those—those monsters!" Mr. Rupert says angrily. He takes a red pen from his pocket and draws an F at the top of Cedrick's quiz.

"Good thing this isn't real school or I'd be upset," Cedrick says with an edge of annoyance in his voice.

"We'll see what your parents have to say," Mr. Rupert says through gritted teeth.

Cedrick crosses his arms hard over his chest and stares down at the table.

"Mr. Rupert," I say as I answer the final question. "We know you're taking all of this really seriously—"

"Because it *is* serious," he says, cutting me off. "It's not a joke. Not a game. Your knowledge of the Vanquishers and of vampire lore might save your life one day and if any of you have the courage to see this training through as your parents did before you, you will one day use this knowledge to protect the public at large. You need to think of that."

Despite what Mr. Rupert says, I *have* been thinking about that. Back in the day, the Vanquishers passed the monikers and the responsibilities down to someone close to them, usually a family member. Later, when that wasn't always possible, they formed the Wrecking Crew for the training of future Vanquishers. But our parents had made a choice—they didn't want this life for us, and a part of me can understand why. Ever since we realized that vamps were back, it's been nonstop chaos.

Jules rolls their eyes and hands Mr. Rupert their quiz. "Are we done for the day?"

Mr. Rupert looks over Jules's paper and then collects mine.

"We're done for now," he says. He stares down at my paper as me, Ced, and Jules stand up and head for the stairs. "Miss Wilson, I need to speak with you before you go."

Cedrick doesn't even pretend like he's gonna wait for me. Jules lingers on the stairs but Mr. Rupert waves them away and they slowly head upstairs. I turn to face him. He's now seated behind a desk that's really just a plastic folding table.

"Something wrong with my quiz?" I ask.

He marks it with his pen, then holds it up so I can see it. A big A+ is written at the top in red. He hands me the paper.

"I got an A-plus?" I ask, a little surprised. "I thought something was wrong."

"Something *is* wrong," Mr. Rupert says as he leans forward on his desk. "Your friends don't seem to be taking this as seriously as they should."

I hold my hand up in front of me. "Just so you know, anything you tell me, I'm gonna go right back and tell Cedrick and Jules and probably my parents, so yeah. Just want to put that out there."

Mr. Rupert's face is a mask of annoyance. "Right." He leans

back in his chair. "You have a good handle on the lessons we've reviewed so far. You are smart, if not a little naive."

"I don't know what that means but I'm gonna assume you're being rude," I say. On the very rare occasions that Mr. Rupert has been nice to us, I don't let it fool me. There's no way this grumpy old man gets any points with me after everything that has happened since the beginning of the school year. He's always been rude. He thinks my friend Aaron is a monster and isn't afraid to tell us that every time he gets a chance. Even when my parents tell him to chill, it doesn't last long.

Mr. Rupert huffs. "You think I'm rude?"

"Yes," I say.

"You have no idea what I've been through. You have no idea what I've seen." He narrows his gaze at me. "I have my reasons for being firm. You'll come to accept it."

"Or not," I say quickly. "My mom says I don't ever have to accept people being rude to me for no reason."

Mr. Rupert almost says something but quiets himself. I bounce gently on the tips of my toes in anticipation.

Please say something about my mom. I'll run and tell her so fast it'll make your head spin.

"You could be a great slayer one day, Miss Wilson," Mr. Rupert says. "Your attention to detail when we review the histories is always spot-on. Your worksheets are always complete and correct. You could put all those skills to use and become a great Vanquisher."

Something about that doesn't sit right with me. I stare down at the floor.

"And of course that means you'll have to put a stake in Aaron's cold, dead heart." He shrugs like he's not talking about one of my best friends, like he's not talking about Miss Kim's only son. "It will be for the best," he continues. "Trust me."

"I won't ever do that," I say. "Not ever. You can't make me. Aaron isn't a monster. He's my friend."

"You have no idea what he will be capable of," Mr. Rupert says quietly. He has a faraway look in his eyes, like he's thinking about something that bothers him. He shakes his head. "I don't have to force you to end him, Miss Wilson. There will come a time where he will leave you no other choice."

"You're wrong," I say defiantly. "You don't know everything. Just because you're always mad doesn't mean I have to be."

The corner of Mr. Rupert's mouth pulls up. "We shall see, Miss Wilson. We shall see."

I crumple up my graded paper, throw it on the ground, and turn to leave. "I wish sunlight would burn your ashy behind to the ground," I mumble under my breath.

"What's that, Miss Wilson?" Mr. Rupert asks.

"Nothing," I say quickly. I rush upstairs thinking about how if sunlight really could do to Mr. Rupert what it does to vampires, his dusty butt would go up in flames.

I join Cedrick and Jules in the front yard where my dad is putting the finishing touches on our new gate—it's made of painted silver and closes our driveway off right near the street. It reminds me of the big gate that closes in the *Addams Family* house. Ours isn't sentient as far as I know. It doesn't move on its own or boot out unwanted guests if it feels like it but it's almost like that, in a way. No vamps are getting past that except Aaron and even for him, it's dangerous.

"Looks good!" my dad says as he steps back and admires the glinting flourishes, the swirls of silver painted charcoal black. "It's perfect."

Cedrick gazes in the direction of his house. His dads put up a new gate, too. Solid silver. More modern looking, though, with its straight up-and-down pickets and level crossbeams. Jules's mom, Miss Celia, opted out of putting up a gate but had a thick band of silver run directly underneath the driveway in a shallow trench. It's covered by dirt and cement, and a vamp wouldn't stand a chance walking over it—or at least that's what our parents have been telling us.

Since our confrontation with the vampires that had come after they attacked me and Aaron and his mom, Miss Kim, things have been quiet—too quiet. Our parents, who are all that are left of the fabled band of masked vampire slayers called Vanquishers, have fortified our houses, our yards, our lives, in anticipation of another attack from this newly formed hive of the undead but so far, it's been crickets. My mom says she's been feeling like she felt when she was still vanquishing, like the silence from the hive is building up to something awful. For me, that awful thing had already happened—my friend Aaron was bitten by a vamp the night of our school fundraiser at the Royal Roller Rink and nothing had been the same since. Finding out my parents and the family members of my closest friends were the legendary Vanquishers was a shock. Almost as shocking as watching Aaron complete his transformation into a creature we are supposed to fear above all else.

Cedrick nudges me with his shoulder. "What did old man Rupert want?"

I sigh and shrug. "Who knows? He's always just running his mouth about nothing. He told me that if I want to be a Vanquisher one day, I'll have to stake Aaron."

Jules rears back like they're absolutely disgusted. "He really said that? What is his problem anyway?"

"I think it has something to do with the vamps," I say.

"I mean, yeah," Cedrick says, shrugging. "He hates them."

"Exactly," I say. "It's not just that he's scared or wants to keep us safe or whatever. He *hates* vampires. Like, it's personal."

"Maybe a vamp scared him when he was little," Jules suggests, pushing their long braid behind their shoulder. "It's gotta be something like that, right?"

"It's gotta be," I say.

"He's a school counselor," Cedrick says. "Can he, like, counsel himself or something?"

I take my phone out and check the FangTime app I'd installed. The name is corny as heck but it tells me the exact moment the sun will set, which tonight is 8:11 p.m. "I don't care about him right now. I just wanna see Aaron."

"Me too," says Cedrick. "We need to watch *Black Panther.*"

"Again?" Jules asks.

Cedrick's brows push together. "Yes. Again."

High above us, storm clouds gather and blot out the already fading daylight. A chill runs through me. I glance at the time—it's seven.

"Everybody inside," my dad says, his tone serious.

I march up the front steps and Jules and Ced follow me inside. We sit side by side on the couch, watching the minutes tick by. I snap a pic of Cedrick through a filter that makes him look like he's got on winged eyeliner and red lipstick. I turn it around and show it to him.

"Not even gonna lie," he says. "It's a good look on me. Send it to me?"

I send it to him in a text and save a copy so I can add it to my latest photo album. It's only about halfway full right now, mostly pics of me and Jules and Ced just acting up, being ridiculous. I have some good shots of my mom and dad, and even a few of Aaron before he, well, before he turned into a vampire. I'm suddenly a little sad.

"What's wrong?" Jules asks, scooting in close to me. "You look upset."

My mom eyes me carefully as I confide in Jules.

"I was just thinking about my photo albums. I have a bunch

of pics of us from before, you know? I want Aaron to be in the new ones I take but he won't show up in them."

"I already got that covered," Cedrick says.

"What?" I ask. "How?"

Cedrick clicks around on his phone and then turns the screen toward me and Jules.

Jules tilts their head. "Is that, like, one of those inkblot tests? Where everybody sees something different? I see a cat with a human face."

I squint hard at the photo and realize it's a drawing Cedrick has taken a picture of. I let my gaze wander up to Cedrick's face to find him grinning, waiting for me to say something.

"Ced," I begin carefully. "Did you—is this—is this a self-portrait?"

"What?" Cedrick asks, confused. "'Course not."

A rush of relief washes over me.

"It's my dad," he says, beaming.

Jules stands straight up and walks away. I try not to look at the portrait because I'm afraid I'm gonna laugh and I don't want to hurt Ced's feelings.

"Why did you draw this?" I ask, trying not to sound like he committed some kind of unforgivable crime.

"Aaron can't show up in pictures," he says. "I know you like to take pictures of all of us so I thought, 'Hey, just do like they did in olden times. Paint a portrait!'" He grins even wider. "It needs some work, but I'm getting better. I'm gonna be painting like Leonardo DiCaprio in no time."

Jules makes a noise like they're choking to death and I glance over to see them and my mom leaning on each other, their backs to us, bodies heaving with silent laughter.

"I think you mean Leonardo da Vinci," my dad says as he saunters over. "Don't let these haters get to you, Ced. I'm sure you—" He catches sight of the drawing still lit up on Cedrick's phone and stops midsentence. "You just keep working on it, Ced. Just keep working."

The doorbell rings and Ced slides his phone into his pocket. My mom lets Miss Celia and 'Lita in. 'Lita kisses me on the top of my head before settling into my dad's recliner. She grips the handle of her retractable silver sword. The blade isn't deployed . . . yet.

Mr. Ethan and Mr. Alex show up next and even though he's annoying, Mr. Rupert also shuffles in looking like he hates the world and everyone in it. When we're all inside, my mom and dad move through their nightly lockup routine, which now includes turning on specialized UV lights in the backyard. They cast a hazy purple glow over almost every square inch of the space and it streams through the kitchen window. The smell of fresh garlic and wet metal permeates the air. Applying vampire repellant to all the windowsills is an everyday task now, even if it leaves the place smelling a little too much like musty armpits.

My dad slides a double deadbolt into place at the front door and posts up by the fireplace near the hidden compartment that holds his silver stakes. Mr. Ethan's index finger is hooked through his belt loop. As he shifts from one foot to the other, his shirt comes up a little and I spy a silver-infused rope hanging around his waist. My mom is much less subtle. She's not pretending she isn't Carmilla anymore, the right hand of the Mask of Red Death. She holds her crossbow close to her chest, her fingers ready to let loose a silver-dust-filled stake at any moment.

We all huddle together in the living room as the alarm on my phone goes off, alerting me that it's time for Aaron to get up. It's a recording I found on YouTube of some man chanting, "I vont to suck your blood!" over and over again. Mr. Rupert replaces his angry face with an even angrier face as I struggle to silence the alarm.

Jules presses their shoulder against mine but we don't make eye contact. If we do, I'll bust out laughing and Mr. Rupert might lose it completely. As we settle into an awkward silence, my mom slowly raises her crossbow and aims it at the front door, finger hovering over the trigger.

My phone buzzes. It's Aaron.

AARON: Hey Boog.

ME: I can't wait to see you! Come over. We're all waiting.

AARON: Already here.

There's a gentle rustling at the front door. My dad's body tenses as he palms a silver stake. Mr. Ethan lets his silver-infused rope unfurl and he crouches low to the floor. 'Lita just holds her little silver stick, letting her thumb rest against the button that will eject the blade of her sword from its hiding place. Miss Celia moves behind the couch and puts her hand on Jules's shoulder. The adults move like a team, and they are. They've fallen right back into a familiar pattern. The Vanquishers are at the ready.

There's a knock at the door.

"It's us," a voice calls. "Kim and Aaron."

My dad goes to the peephole and peers out. He glances back at my mom and she gives a quick nod. He unlocks the door and pulls it open.

Outside the sky is dark, the cicadas are screaming, and my friend Aaron is standing next to his mom on my front porch.

"You can come in," I say.

"You've already invited him in once," my mom says gently. "You don't have to do it every time."

"The invitation stands until you revoke it," Mr. Ethan says. "Only the person who gave the invitation can rescind it, though. Remember that."

I nod. "I didn't even know you could take back the invitation," I said. There's so much more to all of this than I'd realized. All the little details, the ins and outs of vampire lore, it's a lot to think about and a single mess-up could put us all in danger. I wonder if this is how my parents had been living all these years, just trying their best not to make a mistake. In the back of my mind, I know it's the reason my parents are making me attend Mr. Rupert's little classes. I know the information is important. I just wish the person delivering it wasn't such a weirdo.

Aaron steps inside, keeping his eyes low, his head down. He brushes past my dad with a little nod and I bum-rush him. I wrap my arms around Aaron's lanky frame. Chilly air clings to him, like's he's just come in from the cold and not an eighty-five-degree almost-summer evening. He hugs me back and that's where the warmth is. He's still my friend and I don't care what Mr. Rupert says. I'll never do anything to hurt him. Jules and Ced come up and hug him, too.

"How did you . . . sleep?" I ask.

Aaron grins. "Like the dead."

We all bust out laughing and the weird feeling in the room eases up a little. I move around and give Miss Kim a big hug. She pushes my braids behind my shoulder and smiles at me.

"Glad you're here, baby," she says. She squeezes Jules's shoulder. "All of you. It's so good to see—" She stops midsentence as Mr. Rupert clears his throat for no reason.

"Are you sick?" Cedrick asks, knowing that's not the case at all. "Maybe you should wear a mask."

Mr. Rupert's face is stuck in a permanent scowl. His gaze moves to Aaron and then to me. When he looks at Miss Kim, his eyes widen and he takes a half step back. Miss Kim is mean mugging him something fierce. A part of me hopes Mr. Rupert will test her because I'd like to see Miss Kim fold him up one good time. I bet she could do it, too.

"Mr. Rupert is on his way out," I say to Miss Kim.

"I think I'll stay if that's all right with you, Samantha," Mr. Rupert says, glancing at my mom.

My mom shrugs. "Sure. As long as you're on your best behavior, Daniel. Do not start no mess in my house. I'll put you out myself."

I grab Jules's arm and squeeze it. I thought Miss Kim folding him up would be great but if my mom does it, that would be even better. Mr. Rupert sits on a stool by the kitchen and says nothing.

I pull Aaron over to the couch and we sit down together. Cedrick squeezes in and takes out his phone. Him and Aaron gush over leaked set photos from some new superhero movie and they start trading theories and ideas about what the next *Black Panther* movie is gonna be about. Me and Jules exchange glances. We both know we have to let them have their little fanboy moment before we can move on to anything else. Cedrick tries to slide past the drawing that's supposed to be his dad but Jules won't allow it. They reach over and swipe back to the drawing.

"Cedrick is gonna do a painting of you," Jules says. "He's been practicing."

Aaron's lips scrunch up under his nose and his eyebrows push up. "Uh. What's this a drawing of? Is it a werewolf?"

"It's my dad," Cedrick says, swiping the picture off his screen.

"No it's not," Mr. Alex says. "Must be Ethan 'cause ain't no way—"

Mr. Ethan nudges Mr. Alex in the ribs. "It's a masterpiece, Ceddy," Mr. Ethan says. "I love it and I believe in you."

Cedrick beams.

"Just one big happy family," Mr. Rupert grumbles.

'Lita angles her head from her perch on my dad's recliner and glares at Mr. Rupert through her long eyelashes. "Sam has warned you, Daniel. She was much more gracious than I will be if you continue."

Mr. Rupert stands up and clutches his hands together in front of him. "I just—I'm having a very hard time here." His mouth is drawn tight, his eyes narrow. "You all have spent your lives vanquishing for the greater good, fighting the undead at great peril to yourselves and your family, your community. And now, *now*, everyone is suddenly fine with inviting a vampire into your homes? Into your lives? I cannot fathom it."

"He might be a vampire but he's our friend," Jules says. "We keep saying that to you and you don't seem to get it. Is that because *you* don't have any friends, Mr. Rupert?" Jules doesn't say it like they're trying to dig at him. They're genuinely asking and it's something I haven't thought about at all. I wonder if Mr. Rupert has anyone the way I have Ced and Jules and Aaron.

"I understand perfectly," Mr. Rupert says with a quiet anger. "What I understand is that everyone here is willing to throw away generations of tradition for what? For the sake of some ridiculous middle school friendship?"

Mr. Ethan stands up from the dining room table but Mr. Alex pulls him back to sitting. My dad approaches Mr. Rupert.

"Daniel, we know this is hard for you—with everything you've been through—"

"Don't," Mr. Rupert says as tears stand in his eyes. "Don't do that. This isn't the time or place."

I stare into his face and I see something there that's not just pure old-man rage. It almost looks like sadness, like somebody hurt his feelings—bad. My mom slowly approaches him now.

"Daniel, I need you to listen to me. If you can't get on board, you'll have to go." Her tone is gentle but there is no mistaking that she's dead serious. "I can't blame you if you want to take that as an out. I will not hold that against you because I love you like a brother."

Me, Ced, Jules, and Aaron exchange glances.

My mom smiles warmly at me. "A stubborn, hardheaded, obnoxious older brother." She turns her full attention back to Mr. Rupert. "But our goal from here on out is to help Aaron because he is a child and you of all people should understand how precious his life, despite this change in him, is."

"There is no way those two vamps we killed are the only ones out there," my dad chimes in. "Someone made them and I know your commitment to the people of San Antonio is as strong as your commitment to us. We need to find out who bit Aaron and more importantly we need to find out why."

Mr. Rupert's shoulders roll forward and he nods. I don't know if that means he's on board but for now, my mom touches his shoulder and he retakes his seat in silence.

"Are you coming back to school?" I ask Aaron. "You probably can't, huh?"

"There's no way that can happen, Boog," Miss Kim says. "He can't be up in the daylight and even if he could"—she gives Aaron a tight smile—"we just can't risk it. He'll be doing online school for now."

Jules stifles a giggle. "Imagine you're a vampire and you still gotta go to school and do homework." They pat Aaron on the back. "That sucks. I really wish you could be there with us. Only thing getting me through algebra is knowing y'all are gonna be there after class."

Aaron sighs. "I miss that but I can't even keep my eyes open in the daytime so it probably wouldn't work anyway."

"And what do we tell everybody else?" I ask, looking to my mom and dad. "I mean, people know Aaron's been found safe. The rumor is he ran away and then got scared and came back."

Miss Kim bristles. "I hate that that's what people are saying but it's as good a cover story as any. I don't mind letting people believe it."

My mom gives her a quick hug. "I think the general public have accepted that story but the general public isn't exactly who I'm worried about."

I turn to my mom and she's got her lips pressed together, her brow furrowed. Something's up. I'm about to ask her what it is when 'Lita chimes in.

"There are more of the undead out there," she says. "We have to find out what they want, what their goal is. And we must protect Aaron, at all costs." Her steely gaze flits to me and I see nothing but the 'Lita we all know and love—our resident grandma who would do anything to keep us safe. Now Aaron is under her protection, too, and that makes me feel a little better about everything. "We'll keep up the cover story for Aaron," she continues. "But I am wary of warning the public that a hive is now active in San Antonio."

"It's been so long," says Mr. Ethan. "I don't even know how people would react."

Miss Celia shakes her head. "People will do what they always do when they're afraid or when they don't understand something. They'll panic."

"But we can't just leave people unaware of what's happening," Mr. Alex says. "It's already dangerous."

"Rumors are spreading," Mr. Ethan says as he gently puts his hand on Mr. Alex's shoulder. "And not like before when it was some nameless, faceless person in some Podunk town supposedly getting bit. People are wondering what's happening right here in San Antonio. Vampire-proofing supplies were wiped out at H-E-B a few days ago."

"Maybe the rumors are enough to raise people's guards for right now," says 'Lita. "But no formal announcement or anything like that for the time being." Everyone nods in agreement. 'Lita sighs and looks down into her lap. "I wish Dayside was still with us. She always had a way with the toughest situations."

I look to my mom and watch as her expression changes from concern to sadness. "She really did," my mom says. "Nat, too. She would have a plan for this. She was always thinking ahead."

"It would do us all good to remember why they're not here anymore," says Mr. Rupert. "We deal in monsters." He looks Aaron dead in the eye. "There is no planning for anything other than the inevitable."

"Which is what?" I ask. I can't stop myself.

Mr. Rupert folds his hands in his lap. "Monsters will act monstrous. That is a proven fact."

I wish inviting mortals into your house had the same rules as vampires. I'd take back the invitation for Mr. Rupert so fast.

Jules leans in close to me. "I hate the way he's always singling Aaron out," they whisper. "I know he's a vamp but geez. He was our friend first."

I nod and step between Aaron and Mr. Rupert. My mom watches my every move but allows me to say what I need to say.

"Dayside and Nightside aren't here because a vampire killed them. I know that's really hard for you. Y'all were really close." I stare Mr. Rupert right in the face. "But the vampire that did that isn't this vampire." I gesture to Aaron. "Maybe it would do *you* some good to remember that, too, Mr. Rupert." I parrot back Mr. Rupert's own words and I know it's borderline disrespectful but it's too late now.

My dad makes a sound and when I turn to look at him, he's beaming. He walks over and puts his hand on my shoulder, giving it a squeeze. "Boog said it perfectly. Let's not forget where we came from. We owe that to Dayside and Nightside. But let's also try to remember where we're going and how we plan to get there."

"I think we could all use some rest," my mom says. She glances at Aaron. "Even you, baby. How are you feeling, all things considered?"

Aaron shrugs. "Not too bad. Look at this." He raises his arm, and in the low light of the living room lamp, it turns to wispy ribbons of black mist. It stretches toward me and encircles my wrist. Mr. Rupert tenses up, like he might leap from his seat at any moment. I ignore him and the smoke interlaces its tendrils with my fingers.

"It's cold," I say. "Like ice."

"Well, I mean technically I'm dead," says Aaron. "It makes sense that I'd be ice cold."

Miss Kim's mouth turns down and she hugs herself around the waist. Aaron notices and we both move toward her at the same time, wrapping her up.

"Sorry, Mom," Aaron says. "I was tryna make a joke but it's not funny."

Miss Kim waves us off, batting at her eyes. "No, it's okay.

I want you to joke. The fact that you can find anything funny right now is a little bit of a bright spot, right? After all you've been through?"

Aaron nods and his mom squeezes him tight. A knot crawls up my throat. When Aaron was missing, when we thought the worst had happened, it was like a weight was pressing down on all of us. Now he's back and we're all grateful, but he *is* changed. He's a vampire now and a group of people whose only goal was slaying the undead is trying to find a new way of doing things that includes keeping him safe.

When Aaron and his mom leave, they're accompanied by Mr. Ethan and Miss Celia. They're going to do our new and improved lockup routine over at Aaron's while my mom and dad repeat the process at our house. I thought the lockup routine we had before was annoying, but it has nothing on the way we do things now. There are UV lights in every corner of our yard and hanging from every corner of the house, and they can be switched on or off whenever we want. Aside from the new and improved silver gate at the end of our driveway, all our house's exterior doors are either set inside silver doorframes or contain silver in the core of the door itself. The front yard and backyard are now covered with dirt from VDS, the company that supplied graveyard dirt to homes and businesses back in the day. My mom had more holly trees planted and my dad installed thermal cameras. Vamps can't be seen by regular cameras but their cold, dead signatures show up on the thermal cameras, which detect abnormally hot or cold spots. All of this is to keep us safe but there is a part of me that wonders how long it can last. I watched my parents vanquish the vamps that had come after me and Aaron and Miss Kim but there are more. There have to be. And that is the scariest part of all. That a new group of the undead are out there, right now, and they have me and all the people I care about most in their sights.

CHAPTER 2

The next day, Aaron is tucked away in his underground resting place, but I send him a text anyway.

ME: Text me as soon as you get up.

"We still don't know who bit him," Cedrick says, peering down at my phone. "I mean, now it kinda feels like we've got bigger problems, right?"

"Yes and no," I say as we cut across my driveway and make our way to Ced's house. "We should still try to find out. I still think it's important. But yeah. Now we have Mr. Rupert's makeshift Vanquisher training school and we know a bunch of vamps are lurking somewhere close by. And on top of all of that, we gotta keep Mr. Rupert away from Aaron."

Jules shakes their head. "He's just so angry. There's gotta be something else going on with him. What do you think it is?"

I shrug. "I don't know, but my dad always says that just because you're hurt doesn't mean you get to hurt other people. Whatever is going on with Mr. Rupert, I hope he figures it out, and soon, because I'm sick of his attitude and the way he treats Aaron."

We pile into Cedrick's house and take off our shoes. It always smells like some kind of freshly baked goodness in his house, and sure enough, I catch a glimpse of Mr. Alex setting a tray of grilled cheese on the counter.

"Don't even ask," Mr. Alex says, grinning. "Come grab you some."

We consume no less than seven grilled cheese sandwiches between the three of us as Mr. Ethan and Mr. Alex sit and crack jokes about how we never even asked what kind of cheese it is. Apparently, it's cashew-based. I don't care. It's delicious. But Cedrick looks like he's been betrayed by his parents' vegan recipes one too many times.

"I'm glad you're all here," Mr. Ethan says. "We wanted to talk to you about something."

I put my sandwich down and look at Mr. Ethan. "Are we in trouble?"

Mr. Alex laughs and pats my hand. "No, Boog, you're not in trouble." He turns to Cedrick. "You, on the other hand, might be."

Cedrick pushes his plate away and puts up his hands. "The toilet was clogged when I went in there and it's not my fault the plunger broke. I'm not the boo-boo bandit!"

Mr. Ethan's eyes go wide. "Cedrick Anthony Chambers, please tell me you did not destroy another toilet in this house."

"Ummmmmmm, what?" Jules asks. *"Another* toilet?"

"The boo-boo bandit?" I ask, trying really hard not to choke on my cashew-cheese sandwich as I laugh so hard I almost start crying.

Cedrick shakes his head defiantly. "We don't need to talk about either of those things. Ever. For any reason."

Mr. Alex is trying his best not to laugh but he can't help it. He chuckles as he pats Ced on the shoulder. "This isn't about the toilet, Ceddy, it's about the books in the basement."

Cedrick's face goes blank.

Mr. Ethan narrows his eyes at him. "Please, just tell me the book is safe."

I hold my breath. We had borrowed an old book from Cedrick's basement because it had information about vampires and Vanquishers. We hoped it would help us find out how to identify the vamp who bit Aaron, but we hadn't returned it yet.

"It's in my room," Cedrick says as he looks down into his lap.

Mr. Alex lets out a long, slow breath and his shoulders roll down. "Oh, thank goodness."

"I'm sorry," I say quickly. I can't let Ced take the blame for this one. "We were trying to figure out how to help Aaron. I asked Cedrick to get the book. It's my fault."

"We're not upset," Mr. Ethan says gently. "It's nobody's

fault. I know it's been an exhausting few months. I know you kids were trying to help your friend and I'm actually really proud of all of you for doing what was right versus what was easy. You could have told us about Aaron and maybe, because of the way we've done things in the past . . ." He trails off and he has a faraway look on his face. "Maybe it would have been different. But it didn't happen that way, and I'm glad."

Mr. Alex closes his hand over Mr. Ethan's. "What matters is that we're here," says Mr. Alex. "Aaron is as safe as he can be, and we'll get to the bottom of who bit him and why there is a new hive trying to establish itself." He suddenly turns to Cedrick. "My main question is, how did you even get into the basement to get that old book in the first place?"

"I know the code to the door." Cedrick says it like it's the most obvious thing in the world.

"Right," Mr. Alex says, rubbing his temple. "Please go get the book so we can put it back and if you want, we'll take you down there so you can understand why it's so important."

"You're gonna let us see what's in the basement?" I ask.

The basement is off-limits. It always has been. That's why Cedrick had to sneak the book out when we were trying to figure out how to help Aaron, and now we're going to get to see it in person. My heartbeat ticks up and a little rush of excitement pulses through me.

"Yes," Mr. Ethan says. "I already ran it by Sam and Celia. It's time."

"Cedrick," Jules says. "Hurry up and get that book. I've been dying to see what's down there my whole dang life."

Cedrick hops up and runs to his room, returning a few moments later with the book in hand. He gives it to Mr. Alex, who looks it over and sighs.

"Come on," Mr. Ethan says. "We'll give you the tour."

Me and Jules trip over each other as we race to the basement door. Mr. Alex reaches for the little keypad next to it but stops.

"You wanna do it, Ced?" he asks.

A little smirk spreads across Cedrick's face. He scoots past me and enters a four-digit code into the keypad. The little light over the door turns green and with a soft *click* it pops open. Mr. Ethan shakes his head.

"Remind me to change the code," he says, giving Cedrick a playful squeeze.

Mr. Alex leads us into the darkened space below. As we descend the stairs a draft of cool air rushes past my face and when we reach the bottom, the lights flicker on. I don't know what I thought I was going to see—maybe a dusty old basement with a concrete floor and bookshelves, maybe a workbench with some of Cedrick's parents' robotic work. They're engineers and I always thought they would have cool gadgets stashed in the basement but what I see is a room that looks a lot like my mom's lab at the university.

The basement is as big as the footprint of Cedrick's house.

Bright lights overhead illuminate the entire space, which has shiny tiles and floor-to-ceiling shelving on all four sides of the room. There are tables with all kinds of unfamiliar tools and half-built robotic devices scattered across them. On the shelves near the back of the room are rows and rows of books.

"Oh man," Jules says as their mouth hangs open. "I knew there was something down here but this is—what exactly is this?"

"It's our workshop." Mr. Alex moves to one of the tables and sits down on a high stool. "We craft weapons here. Well, Mr. Ethan does."

Mr. Ethan goes over and puts his hand on Mr. Alex's shoulder. "Please give yourself a little more credit. I couldn't do any of this without you." Mr. Ethan turns to us. "When the Vanquishers retired none of us were able to let it go completely." He pauses for a moment. "Old habits die hard, I guess. Miss Celia and I made the weapons for the Vanquishers with knowledge passed down to us from the Vanquishers who came before us, and we improve upon established techniques when new or better tech is available."

"You've been passing this stuff down the whole time?" I ask.

Mr. Ethan nods. "It's kind of a tradition. Whoever inherits the title of Sailor's Knot has to take up the role of weapons crafting as part of that identity. That was a huge part of my job. Each Vanquisher had a role to play and each role was vital." He holds up the book Cedrick had taken from their collection and motions for us to follow him to the back of the room where two large display cases are positioned. Behind the glass panes are books almost identical to the one Cedrick had gotten for us. It takes everything in me not to try and open the glass and read through the rest of the books.

Mr. Alex takes the book from Mr. Ethan and slips it back into the case. "At some point, the original Vanquishers realized that they would not be able to vanquish all of the undead in their lifetimes and that they would have to pass on everything they'd learned to the next generation of Vanquishers so they could keep up the fight," Mr. Alex says. "They kept meticulous notes and these handwritten accounts are an important part of Vanquisher history."

Cedrick looks down at the floor. "I shoved a priceless book written by the original Vanquishers into my backpack right next to some Funyuns and a can of soda."

Mr. Alex cringes but quickly recovers and gives Cedrick a hug. "It's safe now, Cedrick. Don't worry about it."

"Can I—can I read these?" I ask. We'd basically stolen one of the volumes already so I feel weird asking but Mr. Ethan smiles.

"Of course," he says. "Anytime, Boog. Just let me know."

"Can I read that one?" I ask, pointing to the newest-looking edition.

Mr. Alex and Mr. Ethan exchange glances.

Mr. Ethan reaches inside the case, plucks the book from

the shelf, and slips it into my hands. "There are no restrictions on knowledge in this house and y'all are a little too smart to keep much of this stuff from you for too much longer anyway."

I clutch the book to my chest and think about leaving the basement to start reading but something catches my eye. "What's that?" I ask as my gaze drifts to a different display case. This one has a sturdy-looking padlock on it and inside is a single object. The thing resting on the glass shelf inside looks like a thin piece of rope. Light glints off silvery flecks threaded through its coiled length.

Mr. Ethan puts his hand on my shoulder. "That is a piece of the silver-infused rope carried by the original Sailor's Knot. He spun it himself around 1850."

I press my face to the glass to get a better look. "We haven't learned about this stuff yet. I mean, I know that Sailor's Knot carried a silver-infused rope and that vamps hate knots, but that's all they tell us in school."

"And what about Mr. Rupert?" Mr. Ethan asks. "Has he gotten into anything deeper than that with you?"

Jules shrugs. "He mostly talks about how much he hates vamps."

"I'll have a conversation with him," Mr. Ethan says as he turns his attention back to the glass display case with the frayed piece of rope inside. "Vampires had been in existence for hundreds, maybe thousands of years prior to the official formation of the Vanquishers. In the early 1800s vampire numbers were small, but the few of them that were left started coming to the Americas. Here, they used their power to put themselves in positions of influence. They became politicians, church leaders, and landowners." Mr. Ethan's eyes narrow. "Then, in about 1850, right around the time the Vanquishers were forming from disjointed groups of slayers, there was an incident that changed everything."

A look of sadness is stretched across Mr. Ethan's face.

"What happened?" Jules asks.

Mr. Ethan takes a deep, wavering breath. "This is 1850 and our people, Black people, were still enslaved throughout much of the US but there were places where free people had homes and communities. One night, a vampire attacked a family in one of these communities and the people, familiar with the undead, retaliated by hunting down the vampire in the daylight hours and destroying him." Mr. Ethan's eyes glass over and he presses his lips together. "It wasn't easy because the vampires had daytime helpers. Like Renfield from *Dracula*. They called them familiars and they helped keep vampires safe during the day."

"Slayers hunted them down anyway?" I ask.

"Yes," Mr. Ethan continues. "But if you were Black, you couldn't kill a white man even if he was a literal monster, even if he was a vampire. So, the slayers that destroyed the vampire who killed that family were themselves hunted down and well . . ." He glances back at the display case. "They paid a terrible, terrible price."

"The slayers were saving people, though," Cedrick says, as his eyes fill with tears. "They killed a vampire. They were saving people, right?"

"They were protecting themselves and their communities but that didn't matter," says Mr. Ethan quietly. "From that point forward, our people donned masks to protect ourselves and our identities. They kept slaying, and they took the objects that had been used to hurt us and turned them on the undead."

I look at the decaying piece of rope coiled behind the panes of the glass display case and feel a terrible sadness in the pit of my stomach—an ache that I don't have a name for. It's like I'm feeling the sadness and fear that the people who came before me must have felt, and it's so heavy it makes me wonder how Mr. Ethan or any of the other Vanquishers are able to bear it.

Jules puts their hand on my arm and bats tears from their eyes. Mr. Ethan pulls Jules close and gives them a big hug. Mr. Ethan stands in front of me and levels his face with mine.

"We have to remember what happened before so that we can make sure it doesn't ever happen again. We have to be honest about the stories we tell ourselves." He wraps me up in a big, warm hug. "It's a lot to process all at once. Trust me. When I learned the histories myself, not the propaganda pushed out by the wider world, I cried for days. It's okay and you can talk to us or your parents or 'Lita at any time about any of this if you need to." It makes me feel a little better to know he felt the same way I do at one point. "How about we go upstairs and I make y'all some sweet tea? Sound like a plan?"

We all nod and head upstairs. I'm the last one up. I linger at the bottom of the steps, staring back at the display case for a long time before joining everyone in the kitchen.

That night, I read through the handwritten accounts of the Vanquishers in the book Ced's dads let me borrow as we wait for Miss Kim to bring Aaron over. The dates line up with the time leading up to the Reaping. In the days before the final confrontation, my mom and the others tracked the last remaining hive to the Natural Bridge Caverns, where they lit a fire and smoked the undead out of their makeshift crypt. There are entries written by my mom, by Miss Celia, and by Mr. Ethan, but they are short, sometimes just a sentence or two. The feeling is that they're rushed, that they're scared, and that they're running out of time. It's so similar to how I feel right now that I have to put the book down.

Miss Kim's been really nice about letting Aaron come over almost every night even when we have school next day. Tonight, Jules and Ced are at home with their parents and I'm on the couch with my mom while my dad is at work. I don't know where Mr. Rupert is but a part of me thinks he's somewhere powdering the top of his shiny bald head and hopefully thinking about how not to be a complete jerk the next time he comes over.

Mom's got the news on and there's some man talking about the strain the coming summer heat will put on the power grid. My mom heaves a heavy sigh.

"The Texas power grid is held together with bubblegum and duct tape," she huffs. "What if something happens? They just let that thing fall apart and now look, boom. One heat wave or cold snap and everybody's at risk."

Mom has a habit of going off about some random thing when she's upset about something else. I rest my head on her shoulder.

"Wanna talk about it?" I ask.

"Talk about what, baby?" she asks.

I look up at her. Her eyebrows are pushed together and her lips are pressed into a tight line.

"Did you know you have the worst poker face of anybody I've ever met besides Cedrick?"

Mom looks down at me. "Is it that bad?"

"Yup." I snuggle in close to her and she puts her arms around me. "I don't know. There's a lot of stuff going on and you look like you're thinking real hard about something."

"I do have a lot on my mind but you don't need to worry yourself about it," she says.

"I've been reading the entries in the journal Mr. Ethan and Mr. Alex let me borrow," I say.

My mom nods. "It's heavy."

"Yeah it is," I say. "It was really scary, wasn't it? You seemed so scared . . . That's kind of how I feel now."

My mom pulls me close to her and kisses the top of my head. "I was, but I got through it the same way we'll get through this. By keeping our eyes up, being smart, and trusting our instincts." The last word she speaks is clipped and she slides her hand to the handle of the crossbow that now never leaves her side. A glinting silver stake is queued up and ready to go.

My mom eases herself to the edge of the couch, then stands and positions her body between me and the front door. I hold my breath and listen. A few seconds later footsteps sound on the porch and my mom releases her grip on her weapon.

"It's Aaron and Kim," she says, moving toward the door.

"How'd you know?" I ask, standing up. "I didn't even hear anything."

She smiles at me. "Instincts. Remember that."

She pulls open the door and Aaron follows Miss Kim inside. I get ready to give Aaron a hug but he holds his hands up in front of him.

"Wait there," he says, grinning. "I wanna show you something."

"I've seen your smoky arm trick," I say, laughing.

Aaron closes his eyes and before I can blink, he's gone. My mom inhales sharply.

"Where'd he go?" she asks as her gaze darts around the room.

Aaron suddenly reappears directly next to me, but he's panting and has to lean over to rest his hands on his knees.

"Were—were you just invisible?" I ask, stunned.

"Yeah," he says through gasping breaths. "But I can only do it for, like, five seconds and it makes me feel like I'm gonna pass out."

I loop my arm under his and guide him to the couch, where we sit down together. I lean close to his ear.

"We are so going to use this power to get snacks and stuff from the kitchen during our next sleepover. Just want you to know that."

Aaron chuckles but he's still panting. If his heart had been able to beat, I think it would probably be racing. He glances up at his mom, who walks over and hands him a water bottle. He chugs it and the liquid inside leaves a red stain on his lips. His dark eyes are suddenly flecked with red and his breathing returns to normal.

"What's in that water bottle?" I ask as I shoot Jules and Ced a text telling them to come over. "I'm guessing it's not Kool-Aid."

"O negative blood," Miss Kim says. "Donated by yours truly." She holds out her arm and in the crook of her elbow is a Band-Aid taped over a cotton ball.

I swallow hard. It catches me off guard for a minute but when I think about it, I'm pretty sure my mom would donate her own blood to me if I was a vamp. It reminds me of what Mr. Rupert said about dealing in monsters. It's true, but not all the way because Aaron isn't a monster. He's a kid just like me and his mom is still taking care of him.

A moment later the doorbell rings and Mom goes to open it. Mr. Ethan drops off Ced and Jules, then leaves to run errands. Jules kicks off their shoes and sits on the floor in front of the couch as my mom locks up behind them. Cedrick and Aaron slap hands and when their palms collide, Aaron makes his hand into a ball of black smoke. Cedrick's eyes go wide.

"Cool!" he says a little too enthusiastically. "I want a weird smoky hand, too."

"Umm, no," I say, laughing at Ced's pouting face.

Jules rests their head on my knee and I smile at them. I'm glad we're all together.

"I hate to bring the mood down," my mom says to Miss Kim. "But has there been an opportunity for him to be . . . hungry?" There's a tone of hesitation in her voice.

Miss Kim shakes her head. "I don't really want to chance it. I keep him fed on donated blood. Mine or the stuff you gave me. Thanks again for that."

My mom nods. "I have access to donated blood through work. So does Tre. I don't think it will be a problem to keep a fresh supply but he may need to learn to hunt, just in case."

"Hunt?" Jules asks. "Like . . . like people?"

Aaron looks like he's gonna throw up. If vampires can even throw up.

"No," my mom says. "Any blood will work. Vampires have been known to subsist on rats, squirrels, other small animals when the situation calls for it."

Miss Kim lets her shoulders relax. "You're serious? How do you know that?"

"I just do," my mom says. There's something in her voice I can't figure out, almost like another thing she's holding back, and I don't like it at all.

I turn to Aaron as he slurps down the remainder of the blood in the water bottle. He tips it toward me. "Want some?"

"I'm good," I say, laughing.

"We could do a little run-through right now," my mom suggests. "The rear yard is fortified pretty heavily but I think it'd be worth it to try it out."

Miss Kim is hesitant. "I don't know, Samantha."

My mom puts her hand on Miss Kim's shoulder. "If I'm being honest, I have a gut feeling that things are going to get worse before they get better. Aaron has to learn to take care of himself." She glances at me. "All the kids do. For Aaron, that means learning to keep himself safe, getting a handle on his power, and learning to keep himself fed if for some reason we get separated."

"Separated?" Miss Kim asks in a whisper.

I don't like how that sounds. What could happen that would make it so that we aren't all together anymore? I try not to think about it too much.

My mom shakes her head. "I really hope it doesn't ever come to that but I'd rather be safe than sorry."

Miss Kim nods in agreement and we all move out onto the back porch.

The sun is below the horizon but there's still a warm purple light brightening the edges of the evening sky.

"Stay on the porch," my mom says. "Go inside if there's any trouble. Understood?"

"Yes, ma'am," me, Ced, and Jules say in unison.

My mom leads Aaron down into the grass as I move to the rail. From there I can see the entire backyard and over the rear fence into the Green. Everything is still and the only noise is the cicadas. Miss Kim sits on the porch step as my mom and Aaron stand facing each other in the yard.

"She's gonna make him hunt something?" Jules asks. "Is that . . . safe?"

"I mean, maybe not?" I shrug. I really don't know.

"Okay, Aaron," my mom says. "You have all these new abilities. They seem really amazing and maybe you're having some fun with them, right?"

Aaron nods.

"That's good, baby," my mom says. "You should get comfortable with them because they're a part of who you are now, but for this, I'm going to ask you to focus." She squares her shoulders and plants her feet firmly, shoulder width apart. "We know who you are. You're Aaron. Newest member of the Squad, a good kid who loves his mom more than anything, and who has made sure my baby, Boog, was protected when I wasn't there."

A knot builds in my throat.

"But you're something else now, too," my mom says quietly. "You're a vampire and with that comes a host of new abilities. I want you to close your eyes and listen."

He does as she says.

"You'll hear my voice, the cicadas, traffic out past the Green," my mom says. "But underneath all of that are the things that only you can hear—the breathing of each living creature in this space, the flow of blood in their veins, the beating of their hearts."

With his eyes closed, Aaron tilts his head back. He's so still he is almost a statue.

"I hear it," he says quietly.

"Good," my mom says. "If you concentrate hard enough, you can differentiate between human sounds and nonhuman sounds. What you're listening for are faster heart rates, quicker blood flow, the patter of small feet. Try it."

Aaron's temples flex and his eyebrows push together. I move closer to the rail, looking down on him as he follows my mom's instructions.

"I—I hear something," Aaron says. His voice is different. It's like two people are speaking at once.

My mom tilts her head and when I follow her gaze I see an opossum scurrying along the top of the fence. As soon as Aaron sees it, his face changes. His jaw falls open and his eyeteeth poke out from under his top lip. I've seen Aaron's face change before but this is different. He's focused, his eyes tracking the opossum's every move. His fingers elongate and transform into claws. He crouches low to the ground, then explodes forward, slamming into the fence.

I jump back as the opossum scurries across the fence and leaps onto the rail of the porch. Miss Kim scrambles to her feet as Jules and Cedrick move behind me. Aaron is suddenly standing on the porch railing, balancing on top of it like a tightrope walker. My heart cartwheels in my chest as I take another step backward. Aaron's head snaps up and he looks me in the eyes. The hair on my neck stands up and a chill runs up my back. Jules squeezes my arm and I can hear Cedrick hyperventilating behind me.

I've been scared for Aaron ever since he was turned but this is the first time I've ever felt scared *of* him.

"Aaron," my mom says. She's on the porch now, her crossbow in her hand but not leveled at Aaron. Her voice is steady and firm. "The opossum, Aaron."

Aaron takes a deep breath, and then snatches the opossum up and disappears into the shadows of the yard with it. When he reemerges, he looks much more like himself.

"You okay?" I ask.

He nods. "Are you?"

I don't know what to say. I don't think I am. Aaron is my friend and I don't want to be afraid of him, but the way he'd looked as he hunted the opossum really scared me.

"You did good," my mom says as she ushers us all inside.

"You should practice a little more when you have the opportunity but I think that's enough for now. How do you feel?"

Aaron gives her a half smile. "I feel like I should be grossed out but I—I feel okay. I feel better actually."

"There's no substitute for the real thing," my mom says. "Even donated blood isn't quite the same. By the time the blood is donated, packaged, or kept on ice for a while, it has begun to decay. There's a slightly spoiled taste to it, right?"

Aaron looks at his mom and then nods shyly.

"Oh," Miss Kim says. "My blood tastes funky to you?" She sighs. "What can I do? I can maybe eat something tasty first—red beans and rice? That was your favorite before."

My mom rubs Miss Kim's back. "It's not your fault. It's just the nature of blood. It's why when he's feeding from a living creature, it's better for him. He *can* survive on donated blood alone if absolutely necessary, but letting him hunt every once in a while will be good for him."

We go into the living room and sit down, where the TV still plays the news channel. Aaron sits next to me and I try to put the images of him hunting the opossum out of my head.

"So let's talk about our sleepover plans," Cedrick says, breaking the tension that had built up between all of us.

"I'm not watching *Black Panther* again," Jules says.

"Yes we are," says Cedrick.

Jules rounds on him. "There are other movies, Ced."

"Like what?" Cedrick asks.

"I don't know, Cedrick!" Jules says, losing their patience. "*Iron Man 3*?"

Cedrick grabs his chest and gasps like he's so offended he can't function. "Why would you say that to me?" he asks. "Have you—have you seen that movie?"

Me and Aaron lean on each other as we laugh ourselves into a fit. The points of his eyeteeth stick out from under his top lip as he cackles beside me. It feels more like normal with each passing moment.

"Quiet!" my mom suddenly shouts.

We all turn to look at her, wondering what we did wrong, but she's not even paying attention to us. Her gaze is fixed on the muted TV screen. The news is still on. She rushes over, snatching up the remote and turning the volume up so loud I have to cup my hands over my ears.

"A string of suspicious disappearances seems eerily reminiscent of days long past," a reporter says. "To a time before the Reaping and before the Vanquishers retired from public service. But officials have assured us that there is no reason to suspect anything is amiss for the time being." The reporter smiles, but I can't help but feel like she's lying.

"Disappearances?" I ask.

The video cuts to a man in a black jacket with a mop of blond hair talking to a reporter.

"I'm sure it's nothing," the man says. "People need to calm down and not panic."

My mom's face is ashen. She almost drops the remote but recovers enough to cut off the TV.

"I know y'all are planning a sleepover but it will need to wait," my mom says in a monotone sort of way. She dials numbers on her phone and one by one, Jules and Ced are collected and Aaron and Miss Kim make their way home.

When my mom and I are alone again, I want to ask her what's happening but I don't want her to lie to me. An eerie silence fills our house as my mom starts the new and improved nightly lockup routine.

CHAPTER 3

Cedrick slides into the back seat of my dad's SUV the next morning.

"What the heck is goin' on, Boog?" he asks. "You saw your mom's face when that news reporter was talking about people disappearing. She thinks it's vamps. I know it."

"She definitely thinks it's vampires," I say. "But what's that mean? They're, like, going on a murder spree? Kidnapping people? What?"

Jules pops the door open and dive-bombs in next to me.

"This is wild, right?" they ask, rubbing their jaw.

"You had to use that little key thing in your mouth again, huh?" I ask.

Jules nods. "It's called a palate expander. It's just supposed to make more room in my mouth but it feels like it's expanding my whole face." They groan and take a deep breath. "Anyway, 'Lita's been watching the news more than her telenovelas and that means something's up."

My dad cuts the music off, then twists around in the front seat so that he's looking directly at us. "Listen," he says. "I know y'all aren't little kids anymore. I know you're hearing things and picking up on stuff, but you're also not grown." He sighs and shakes his head. "I don't know exactly what's happening and neither does anyone else. We have our suspicions."

"Vamps are coming to bite our necks off, huh?" Cedrick asks.

My dad looks like he wants to scream. "We are working to figure it out," he says, bypassing Ced's question. "Is it vamps? Maybe. Probably. But we can't just go saying that. We have to be discreet until we know exactly what we're dealing with."

"Aren't we dealing with vamps?" I ask. "I mean, I know we are." I glance toward Aaron's house and it makes me sad that we can't swing by and take him to school with us.

My dad nods. "We are dealing with the undead, yes. But it seems oddly specific. Why Aaron? Why show up here and confront us? Why not take out other people on our street? Why now? Vamps were never too picky about who they made meals of." He seems like he's just talking out loud, not really expecting answers to all his questions. "Now people are missing," he says with a faraway sound in his voice. "Missing. Not turning up dead with holes in their necks. No. Something else is happening here and we're gonna get to the bottom of it but you all need to keep this information between the three of you."

"Four," I say quietly. "Don't forget Aaron."

My dad's face softens. "Of course not, baby. Keep this stuff between the four of you. That means even when someone is saying something you know isn't true, you have to play it cool. Understood?"

We all nod.

"Promise me," my dad says.

"Promise," I say.

"Vampires don't exist and your stupid friend Aaron made everybody all upset for nothing," Adrianna says as she glowers over me while I sit at my desk. I guess I get to put my dad's advice to the test sooner than I thought I'd have to.

"Okay, Adrianna," I say, rolling my eyes. "He's home. Nothing else really matters." I pick at the end of one of my braids as she continues to huff and puff. Her breath smells like chewing gum and soda and her upper lip is sweaty. She's a mess.

"No. They should arrest Aaron or something. He made everybody worried for no reason and people started talking about—" She stops short, straightening up.

"About vampires?" Cedrick asks from his seat behind me. "Well, they don't exist. You just said it. So what is it? You're scared of vamps or they don't exist—which one is it? Because I'm confused."

Cedrick is done with Adrianna and so am I but we have to play it cool, like my dad said.

Adrianna leans over Cedrick's desk. "You think everything is a joke."

"Not everything," Cedrick says. "Just you."

Adrianna scowls down at Ced, who smiles up at her.

"Adrianna," a voice snaps.

Mrs. Lambert is standing in the doorway, coffee cup in hand, bag slung over her shoulder. "Detention. Go put your name on the board." Her tone is sharp and she looks exhausted.

"What?" Adrianna asks. "Why?"

"Because I said so," Mrs. Lambert says. "You are standing firmly on my last nerve, so I suggest that if you don't want to make it in-school suspension, you do as I say."

Adrianna marches up to the board and angrily scribbles her name in red dry-erase marker, then stomps back to her desk, where she sits down so hard the chair scrapes against the floor. I look to Mrs. Lambert, expecting to see that familiar little smile, but she doesn't meet my gaze.

"Class," she says out loud. "I am having a day. I think it's important to communicate with you all about how I'm feeling. Effective communication is key. Bullying, for example, isn't tolerated." She stares at Adrianna, Leighton, and Emma. "If you are upset, if you are worried, say that. Don't act out. I'm going through some things personally, and I may seem a little down, but I am going to be okay. I just wanted y'all to know."

She digs around in her bag and pulls out a rectangular box,

setting it on her desk where a fly has already made its way onto the lid of her coffee cup. She opens the box and pulls out a cylindrical container with a domed top. The bottom portion is see-through and it's attached to a long power cord that she plugs in behind her desk. A muted blue light emanates from the little dome and it makes a soft *whooshing* sound.

"What is that?" Jules asks.

Mrs. Lambert smiles for the first time since she'd come in. "This is the CatchPro. Watch."

She sits down and becomes still as a statue. The fly on her coffee cup buzzes around the lid a few more times, then zips toward the CatchPro. As soon as it buzzes over the glowing dome, it gets sucked inside and a moment later it reappears in the bottom portion of the contraption buzzing around in circles.

"Cool!" Bradley shouts from the back of the class. "It's a bug trap. Is it gonna die in there?"

"No," Mrs. Lambert says with an edge to her tone. Mrs. Lambert flicks the side of the CatchPro as the fly continues to buzz around inside. "Since admin isn't doing much about the fly infestation, I figured I need to take more drastic measures."

"Why do they keep coming in here anyway?" Leighton asks.

"I wish I knew," says Mrs. Lambert. "Maybe they're attracted to the smell of funk that y'all constantly bring in here." She smiles and I feel better knowing that she seems to be feeling a little more like herself now. "Take out your planners and let's get started."

I pull my folders and planner out of my disaster of a backpack and when I look up, Mr. Rupert is standing outside the classroom door, his face framed in the little glass window.

Cedrick follows my gaze and when he sees Mr. Rupert, he groans.

"I'm sick of him!" he scream-whispers. He flicks his hand in the air, gesturing for Mr. Rupert to go away.

Mr. Rupert's face twists into a mask of pure annoyance and a moment later he's gone from the window.

All day, I hear students talking about the rumors that vampires might be responsible for the recent strange disappearances, but for every person who suggests a vamp, there is someone else who insists it's kidnappers or a cult or something. Students and teachers are talking about Aaron, saying how he ran away and got everybody worried for no reason and I wonder if everybody feels like that and not just Adrianna. Nobody seems panicked or even overly concerned, but my heart beats like a drum the entire day. They don't know what I know and I wonder if this is how the Vanquishers felt having to keep all of this from the world for so long.

My mom picks me, Jules, and Ced up after school and our first stop is Aaron's house. Freshly planted holly trees now line the drive. There is a big no trespassing sign on the gate that leads to the backyard. Miss Kim meets us at the front door—a door that is set inside a new silver-plated frame. She gives my mom a big hug and they do that thing where they both rock side to side while they're caught up in each other's arms. My mom and Miss Kim have become BFFs and it shows.

"I made some sandwiches for y'all," Miss Kim says, giving me a big hug, too. "Aaron isn't really eating . . . sandwiches." There's a long pause and then she sighs. "I still get all his favorite stuff when I go to the store. Just a habit, I guess."

My mom hugs her again. "It's gonna be okay, Kim. One way or the other."

Miss Kim nods. "I haven't made much progress. My home lab setup is great. Thanks for that, Samantha, but it's just not the same as being in a research facility."

"No, I know," says my mom. "I'm afraid if we bring a bunch of stuff here, it'll draw unwanted attention. I know there's still some media sniffing around because of Aaron's reappearance. They're suspicious but I'd like to keep them at bay for as long as possible."

Miss Kim nods. "I wish they'd find something else to fixate on. In the meantime, I'll work with what I've got." She smiles warmly at my mom. "Got a few hours until Aaron's up. Want to see how my setup's coming along?"

"Can we see, too?" I ask. She, like Ced's dads, has her lab in the basement of the house. Mr. Ethan helped her install a security door and black out the little basement windows. We haven't been down there since she locked it up but I've been dying to see what it looks like now.

"I just want to eat," Cedrick says. "Y'all go ahead and look at vampire residue in the basement. I'm good here."

Miss Kim laughs. "Have at it, Ced. But, Boog, sweetie, you can come down if you'd like. You too, Jules."

We leave Ced to stuff his face with turkey sandwiches and chips and follow Miss Kim and my mom into the basement.

As soon as we emerge into the space below, the smell of rubbing alcohol wafts into my face and makes my eyes water. It smells just like the facility my mom works in—like a cross between a hospital and a museum. The back half of Miss Kim's basement is sectioned off with big sheets of plastic duct-taped to the floor and ceiling. They puff in and out as something that looks like a portable air conditioner pushes and pulls air around the room.

"It's cold down here," says Jules as they rub their exposed forearms.

"I have some blood and tissue samples down here," says Miss Kim. "It's best to keep things cool. It's a pretty good setup for now."

"There might be some other options but this looks great for the time being," my mom says.

"So what exactly are you doing down here?" Jules asks, scanning the room. "Are you looking for something specific?"

"I'm hoping to find a way to reverse the change in Aaron completely," Miss Kim says. "I know that I'm nowhere near doing that but in the meantime I'm hopeful I can give Aaron a reprieve from needing human or animal blood and from some of the effects of his exposure to sunlight."

My mom's phone buzzes in her pocket and she takes it out, glancing at the screen. "Hang on one sec. This is my job," she says. She answers it. "Hello? Hey, Steph. Everything okay?" My mom's face suddenly changes and her smile is replaced by a look of deep concern. "How bad is it?" Whatever she hears as the answer to that question makes her sigh and shake her head. "I'm on my way." She hangs up and shoves the phone back in her pocket. "Kim, could you do me a favor and take Jules and Cedrick home? There's been some kind of break-in at my job and I need to go see what happened."

"Of course," Miss Kim says. "Go ahead and do what you need to do. I've got the kids."

My mom nods to me and then she's pulling me out to the car before I can say bye.

"Mom, I can stay with Ced and Jules. I don't need to go."

"Daddy's not home, Boog," she says. "I want you close to me, okay?"

I'm not gonna argue with her. She seems genuinely upset and as we speed out of the neighborhood she takes and makes a flurry of calls.

"A break-in at my lab," she says into the phone. "Yeah. I don't know. I'm on my way. I have Boog. Kim has the other kids. Eyes up. I have a really bad feeling about this."

CHAPTER 4

The San Antonio campus of the University of Texas is a winding maze of intersecting avenues. Tan buildings with terra-cotta-colored roofs line the streets as my mom steers through the labyrinth. We pull up to the medical research building, a more modern-looking structure with a glass portico and automatic doors. I've only been up to my mom's office a handful of times in my entire life. The last time was a few months before Aaron moved onto our block. I always have to sit in the lobby or the break room because most of the areas are off-limits to anybody except staff. What I remember most is the weird antiseptic smell and the too-bright lights.

Right after we park, my mom is rushing me out of the car and inside the building, where the cool flush of AC beats back the sweltering heat. There is a low murmur as we push into the crowded foyer. People in white coats, other people in scrubs, others in khakis and polos are standing around. Everyone is wearing the same look of concern on their faces.

My mom has a death grip on my hand and is pulling me along until she stops suddenly. I run into her and wait for her to chew me out about stepping on her heel, but she doesn't even look back at me. I peer around her to see what the problem is. Two burly men in uniforms that read "Security" across the front are standing guard at the elevators.

"What's wrong?" I ask.

She turns and speaks to me while she scans the rest of the entryway. "The security for this building wear security uniforms just like those men, but the lettering is all capitals. The men at the elevator—look at the lettering on their shirts."

I peer around her, trying not to be obvious. The word "security" is there, but it starts with a capital S while the rest of the letters are in lowercase.

"Also, their hair is brushing the tops of their ears," my mom says just above a whisper. "That's out of regulation for them. Not to mention that in all the years I've worked here, I've never seen these two."

I stare up at her. "So, they're not security?"

She shakes her head. "Not for this building anyway." She scans the room, still avoiding looking at me directly, and when she speaks, her lips barely move. "There's another one near the front door."

I start to turn around to look but she puts her hand on my

shoulder. "I watch your back, you watch mine. What are the ones by the elevators doing?"

My heart kicks up. My mom's Vanquisher skill set clearly is about more than just silver-stake-spewing crossbows.

"They're just standing there," I say. "They look bored."

"Are they looking in our direction?" she asks.

"No," I say.

My mom lets the air hiss out from between her teeth, then gently squeezes my shoulder. I follow her gaze toward a wide hallway to our immediate right. We slowly walk toward it, her hand on my back as we weave through the crowd. Everyone has cleared out halfway down the hall and my mom pulls me into a dimly lit stairwell. A wave of uneasiness ripples through me.

"Isn't your office on the sixth floor?" I ask, my voice echoing off the walls.

The corner of her mouth draws up. "Yes. Let's go."

By the time we reach the sixth floor, I'm sweaty and I have to pull my braids into a lopsided bun on top of my head.

"I think I have shin splints," I say, rubbing the front of my legs.

My mom pats me on the back. "You okay?" She's not even out of breath.

I nod as she pulls her work badge out of her pocket and waves it in front of a little gray rectangular box to the right of the door. There is a soft *click* and she pulls it open.

We enter a long hallway lined with doors adorned with signs that say things like Clean Room and Biohazard Storage. The bright lights overhead hurt my eyes. As we move down the hall, voices ring out.

"It was secure when I left last night," a high-pitched voice says. "And where was security? Have we gotten in touch with them? This is absolutely unacceptable!"

"We've been in touch," a deep voice answers. "We're reviewing their activity as we speak."

My mom stops dead in her tracks and I run into her again. She turns around and grabs me by the arm, leading me into a small room, where she closes the door behind us. She doesn't turn on the light.

"Listen to me very carefully," she says. "I want you to stay here."

"What?" I was kind of enjoying our little lesson in spying on fake security guards. "What's wrong?"

"Something's not right," she says. A worried look spreads across her face, the same look she'd had as we watched the news the other night. "Stay here. You got your phone?"

I pat my pocket. "Yeah."

"Here." She puts her security badge in my hand. "If I'm not back in a few minutes, use it to go out the same way we came in. Call your dad from the car."

"You're scaring me," I say. I hold tight to her hand. "Let's just leave together."

She shakes her head. "It's probably nothing." I don't believe her at all. "Better to be prepared," she says. She turns and leaves, and for a moment I think about just bolting out the door and running back to the car like she told me to. I put my hand on the door and peer out the narrow window. I can't see anything. I push it open a few inches.

"Mrs. Wilson," the deep voice says. "It's good to see you."

"So we're lying now?" my mom asks, her tone sharp. "What are you doing here?"

I open the door a little more and step halfway out into the hall. I still can't see my mom but I'm way too nosy to just ignore her conversation.

"If everyone could please move down the hall and into the reception area, that would be greatly appreciated," a different voice says.

There is a murmur of voices and footsteps retreat toward the other side of the building. I press myself against the wall, right at the corner, and peer around. My mom's office door is wide open and the contents of her bookshelves and desk drawers are spilled across the floor. The glass surrounding a research lab immediately to the left of her office is shattered and the broken pieces glint in the flickering lights. My mom's coworkers have shuffled off. Now it's just her and two people in black coats that have a small symbol on the breast pockets—two concentric circles, one gold and one silver with four solid gold lines protruding from the top, bottom, and sides. It looks almost like a little sunshine.

My mom stands with her back to me and the two men stand in front of her.

"Samples were taken," my mom says. "Vampire flesh, blood, and the bisected corpse."

I inhale sharply but try to keep myself from making any other noise. They really do have vampire bodies here, or at least—they did.

"We know," the taller man with the mop of sandy blond hair says. "Your coworkers informed us." He looks familiar to me but I can't place him.

My mom shifts her weight from one foot to the other. "This has something to do with the undead."

There is a long silence. My heart kicks in my chest. These people know my mom and they know about vamps maybe still being a threat. I keep myself hidden and continue to eavesdrop.

"Looks like a run-of-the-mill break-in to me," says the blond guy.

"You wouldn't be here if that were true," my mom says. "Don't play games with me. I saw you getting your fifteen minutes of fame on the news the other night. Why are you here?"

That's where I recognize him from. He was on the news. I thought he was just some random bystander but as I look at him I recognize the jacket and his hair.

"We knew you'd jump to conclusions," says the other man, the one with black hair and beady little eyes. "We're here to remind you that—"

"I don't need you to remind me of anything," my mom snaps.

"Are you sure about that?" the blond man asks. "Seems like you're already skimming blood bags off the inventory. Some equipment is on loan to you, too. Wouldn't be hiding a freshly turned vamp in your basement now, would you, Samantha? You've always been soft on some of those bloodsuckers, haven't you?"

My mouth goes dry. Blood rushes in my ears. They have to be talking about Aaron. It can't be anybody else, but how? It's a secret only we're supposed to know.

The man with the black hair steps close to my mom and she squares her shoulders at him. As confused as I am, a little swell of pride washes over me. My mom will mop the floor with this guy if he tries anything and I kind of want to see her do it.

"Remember who you are," says the man. "Who you *really* are."

"Give me five feet before I snap your forearm in half," my mom says. My mom leans so close to the man he can probably feel her breath in his face. "I remember exactly who I am. Do you?"

I have to slide my hand over my mouth to keep from hollering. The man backs up and it's crystal clear that he's scared to death of my mom but she was the one who had instructed me to leave if she didn't come back in a few minutes. I don't think she's actually afraid of him but as he straightens out his jacket and runs his hand over the symbol on the pocket, she stiffens. Whatever that symbol represents, *that's* what she's afraid of.

"Nothing has changed," the man says. "We don't want to create a panic now, do we? If you say anything, we'll be forced to put the rumors down. It would be a shame if the public found out retired Vanquishers were conjuring up stories to make themselves relevant again."

My mom turns her head and grits her teeth. "How dare you."

He starts to walk away but looks back over his shoulder at the last minute. "We'll be in touch, Samantha." He and the other man make their way down the hall.

My mom suddenly turns and comes around the corner before I have time to duck away. She stares down at me and her eyes narrow. "How much did you hear?"

No sense lying. "All of it," I say as I grind the toe of my sneaker into the linoleum floor.

My mom huffs. "Come on."

She leads me back down the stairs and out to the car, where the men in the black jackets are piling into a blacked-out SUV.

"Who were those people?" I ask. "What did they want?"

My mom shakes her head. "I don't want to talk about it right now," she says as she starts up the car and we make our way back home.

I slide my phone out of my pocket and send a text to the group chat.

ME: Meet me at my place. Y'all are not gonna believe what just happened.

A few seconds later my phone buzzes.

CEDRICK: What time is Aaron waking up?

JULES: FangTime app says the sun sets at 8:09 tonight

ME: His mom's bringing him over. Probably close to 9

CEDRICK: Will there be snacks?

ME: Takis, juice, and leftovers.

CEDRICK: Say less

CHAPTER 5

As we're speeding home, my mom takes several hushed calls. She pops in a Bluetooth earpiece so that I can't hear whoever is on the other end of the line. She speaks in half sentences and short answers, obviously sounding the alarm while trying very hard to keep the details from me.

"Yes," she says. "Mullins and Davis. Same thing as before."

We turn onto Noble Knight Road as the sun is setting and she pulls into Aaron's driveway. "Pit stop," she says. "I need to talk to Miss Kim."

I don't complain. Cedrick and Jules are still there and I'm dying to see Aaron, so we all decide to wait for him before going back to my house.

"You're stepping on my foot!" Jules yelps as we crowd around Miss Kim's back door and peer through the window.

"Why is your foot so dang long?" Cedrick asks. "Move it over!"

Jules huffs and squeezes between me and Cedrick. I press my face close to the glass to try and get a good view of the shed in Miss Kim's backyard. Aaron sleeps under it during the daytime. Over the past few weeks, our parents had helped Miss Kim turn the area into a sanctuary for Aaron. It was weird watching them build a structure that's meant to keep a vampire safe inside while repelling other vampires that might want to creep up on him.

My dad had ordered a bunch of holy earth from VDS and fortified Miss Kim's property line with it. My dad and Mr. Ethan also reinforced her fence with pickets that contained silver cores and planted holly trees at six-foot intervals around the entire perimeter of the house. Miss Celia also handed over about five gallons of 'Lita's homemade vampire repellant. Miss Kim has to use it sparingly, though, because it works on Aaron, too.

As the sun fades from the sky, me, Ced, and Jules press against the back door's window hoping to catch a glimpse of Aaron emerging from his hiding spot. While we wait, my mom and Miss Kim huddle up in the living room. I angle my head just enough to try and listen in on their conversation.

"Everything was destroyed or taken," my mom says.

"Have you told the others?" Miss Kim asks.

"Yes," my mom says in a hushed tone. "'Lita left immediately. I don't know when she'll be back."

I don't like that at all.

"Look!" Cedrick says suddenly.

My attention snaps back to the shed in the backyard as the doors slowly push open. Like a shadow unfolding from the darkness itself, Aaron emerges, stretching his hands overhead. His jaw unhinges in a wide yawn. In the dark I can just make out the elongated eyeteeth and a chill runs up my spine. He suddenly catches sight of us and readjusts his dangling jaw, glances around, then hops on a pattern of paving stones that lead to the back door. He moves in a very specific way, avoiding some stones, stepping on the edges of others. Mr. Ethan had helped my dad infuse silver and holly shavings into some of them. Aaron knows where to step to avoid them and that's the whole point. Another vampire won't know which ones are protected and would burn their feet right off.

Aaron steps off the last stone and is suddenly standing on the other side of the glass. Both Cedrick and Jules take a step back. Aaron's face is gaunt, his black eyes are swimming with red flecks, and even though he has closed his mouth, his jaw is tilted, like it's not lined up right.

I tell myself over and over that I don't have to be afraid of him. I hate that Mr. Rupert's words of caution are echoing in my head. I push them away.

Miss Kim gently brushes past me and opens the four big deadbolts on the back door. Aaron slips inside and she sweeps him into a hug but he doesn't hug her back.

"What's wrong?" Miss Kim asks.

I love Miss Kim but it feels like a silly question. Your son's a new vampire. He's got a lot going on. But I keep that to myself.

"I'll get you something," Miss Kim says. She disappears down the back hallway, then returns a moment later with a Hydro Flask. She tosses it to Aaron and he smiles gently.

"Wanna go to my room?" Aaron asks.

Cedrick glances at my mom, who stays perfectly still as she watches Aaron. She'd never harm him but every time they're in the same room she watches him intently, like she's studying him. She nods and we march upstairs as Aaron chugs down the blood in the Hydro Flask.

"Is it tasty?" Jules asks.

Aaron nods but doesn't look at Jules. "Yeah. Umm when I first get up, I feel like I could eat a horse."

"You mean drink a horse?" Cedrick asks. "Like, stick a straw in it like a Capri Sun?"

"Do you want to go hunt?" I ask. "I bet there's a bunch of opossums outside right now."

Aaron pauses for a moment. "They *are* tasty but no. I'm good with this for now." He gives the Hydro Flask a little shake.

We pile into Aaron's room. Cedrick plops down at Aaron's desk and me and Jules sprawl out on the rug. Aaron sits on his bed. He doesn't use it anymore, so it's always perfectly made.

Aaron's eyes have almost returned to normal. Only a few thin red flecks swirl in the pupils of his big brown eyes. His face is fuller, more like his old self. He looks almost normal sitting there on his bed, surrounded by Spider-Man posters and piles of comics and rumpled clothes in the hamper. It's all so normal even though we all know there's nothing normal about the situation at all.

"I gotta tell y'all something but you gotta promise that it stays between us for right now," I say in a whisper.

Jules's eyes widen. "This about the break-in at your mom's job?"

I nod and glance toward the open bedroom door. Aaron follows my gaze and before I have time to blink twice, he's up and silently easing the door shut, then sitting so close to me I can feel the cold radiating off him. Cedrick joins us on the rug and we huddle close, keeping our voices low.

"So look, somebody broke into my mom's job," I say in a whisper. "When we showed up there were some security guys there but my mom clocked them immediately. They weren't security at all. They were wearing fake uniforms."

Cedrick's brow shoots up. "What? Why would there be fake security there?"

"I think they were waiting for my mom to show up," I say. "So she takes me up the back stairs and we hear a guy talking to one of her coworkers. She pulls me into a room and tells me that if she doesn't come back, I need to leave and call my dad."

Jules's jaw drops open. "Boog, that's so scary!"

"What happened?" Aaron asks.

"I eavesdropped," I say. "There were two people and one of

them was on the TV the other night saying people were over-reacting about the disappearances. He was there with another dude and they both knew my mom. Like, *knew* her."

"Like, that she's a Vanquisher?" Cedrick asks, his eyes wide.

I nod. "And they said something about her skimming blood bags from her job. They're knee-deep in her business and they know way more than they're telling."

"Why would they be on the news telling people to calm down if they know vamps are still a threat?" Jules asks.

"They're hiding something," I say. "I don't know what, but it's got my mom worried."

"What did your mom say to them?" Jules asks.

"She told the one guy if he got any closer to her she was gonna break his arm in half."

The grin that spreads across Cedrick's face is so wide and cheesy I can literally see all his teeth. "And that's why Carmilla is my favorite."

I smile a little, too. It was a serious threat and my mom meant every single word.

"And did you hear what my mom told Miss Kim downstairs just now?" I ask.

Everyone shakes their heads no.

I lower my voice even further. "My mom said that she told the others, the other Vanquishers, what happened and then 'Lita left."

Jules looks at their phone. "Lita said she had to go do something. She didn't say what, though. She just grabbed her purse and left."

"Our parents are still hiding something from us," I say.

Cedrick huffs. "I thought them being Vanquishers was the big secret."

"Or maybe *one* of their big secrets," I say. "These people at her job knew about her and she seemed like she knew them, too." I pause and then remember the symbol. "And they threatened her. Told her she needed to keep quiet about new vamps or they'd spread a rumor that the Vanquishers were making all this up so they'd be popular again."

"When have the Vanquishers ever not been popular?" Cedrick asks. "Makes no sense."

"They both had on dark clothing," I say. "And on their coats was a symbol that looked like some circles with lines coming out of the sides." I grab a piece of paper and a pen from Aaron's desk and draw the symbol.

"What's it mean?" Aaron asks.

I shrug. "No idea. But we should try to figure it out, right? Why still keep secrets from us?"

"We still don't know who bit Aaron," says Cedrick. "Are we still worried about that? Could this have something to do with it?"

I glance at Aaron, who has lowered his gaze to the floor. I gently put my hand on his shoulder.

"I don't know," I say. "But we're gonna figure that out, too. I promise."

"I don't think it matters anymore," Aaron says quietly. "The change is done. There's no going back now. Even if we find the vampire who bit me, I don't think we can undo this." He holds his hands up in front of him. "My mom says she's gonna try, but I think she's just trying to make me feel better."

We all sit quietly for a while, letting that sink in. He's right, but it feels like he's giving up and I don't want to do that. Not yet.

"Your mom thinks there's still a chance to reverse it," I say. "And even if we can't change it I want to know why. Why you? Why should you have to go through all this?" I bite back tears. "It's not fair and I want answers."

"And maybe some revenge," Cedrick offers.

I think about that. Mr. Rupert isn't teaching us offensive skills but yeah, maybe one day I can stake the vamp who did this to Aaron.

"I don't like the look in your eyes when you talk about getting revenge," says Jules as they stare into Cedrick's face. "You look a little too happy about that being a possibility."

Cedrick just shrugs. "I just wanna learn to fight them."

"I'm a vampire, too," Aaron says. "Don't forget that."

Cedrick goes quiet for a minute, then looks over at Aaron. "I'd never do anything to hurt you. I just want to slice up the vamps that did this to you. I don't think I can ever forget the way your mom's face looked when everybody thought you were, well, when they thought you were dead."

Aaron's face is tight. "You're not wrong. I just don't know how I'm supposed to help when I'm one of them."

"That's the best part," Cedrick says excitedly. "You know what it's like and you can do all the stuff they can do except you're not a monster. You're just Aaron."

"You're Aaron, but sometimes you can turn into a cloud of smoke or something," Jules says.

"And you can disappear and reappear," I say. "And—"

"Okay," Aaron says quickly, biting back a toothy smile. "I get it. I'm not a monster but I can do some monster things."

"Wish I could do monster things," Cedrick sulks. "I wanna turn into a wolf or something."

"I don't think I can turn into a wolf," Aaron says.

"Have you tried?" Cedrick asks.

Aaron thinks for a minute. "No but now I kind of want to."

It's only an hour before my mom is corralling us downstairs and shuffling us into her car while she stands guard. Aaron disappears from the driveway and reappears on the roof where he keeps watch. I keep him in my line of sight until we get to my house and my mom pulls the car into the garage.

She walks Jules and Cedrick home while I stay safely inside the threshold. I don't press her to let me out on the porch anymore. I know what's waiting in the dark and it's nothing to play around with.

When my mom returns, she comes in and goes through the lockup routine as I head off to bed. Late nights with Aaron make me sleepier in the daytime but school's almost out and Aaron needs us. I shower, brush my teeth, and slip a bonnet over my braids before trudging into my room and falling into bed.

Downstairs, the TV clicks on and the news echoes through the hall. Someone is talking about another disappearance.

The school day was long and boring and now our afternoons are long and boring, too. Mr. Rupert is going on and on about the importance of being cautious around Aaron as we wrap up our lesson with him the following day. The only thing helpful I've learned in today's lesson is that 'Lita became the official leader of the Vanquishers in 1990 and Mr. Rupert became the official historian and record keeper for them in the same year. But the thing that kept me on the edge of my seat was the revelation that my mom joined the Wrecking Crew at the age of thirteen. She was brought into it by the woman who held the Carmilla mantle before her and became an expert with the crossbow almost immediately. She took to vampire slaying like fish to water.

"I'll be thirteen in a few months," I say. I can't help but think about what it must have been like for my mom to be in full-on Wrecking Crew mode at almost the same age as me.

What we're doing with Mr. Rupert almost feels like Wrecking Crew lite.

"Your mother was, and continues to be, one of the most capable, intelligent people I've ever met," Mr. Rupert says. "She is a tactician with that crossbow of hers."

Cedrick presses his forehead into the table and groans before sitting straight up.

"Mr. Rupert, please," Cedrick says. "I love hearing all this other stuff"—he glances at me to let me know that he's lying—"but can you teach us at least one thing we can actually use against the vamps? If we have to fight them, they're not gonna want to hear a detailed history of the Vanquishers."

Mr. Rupert's face twists up. "You know vampire rhymes, right? They're a very efficient tool against the undead."

"Seriously?" Cedrick whines. "That's baby stuff. That's not gonna cut it when a pack of undead monsters are breathing down our necks. What am I gonna do, stop and shout, 'Mary, Mary quite contrary, how does your garden grow'?"

Jules looks absolutely bewildered. "Cedrick, what even is that rhyme?"

He shrugs. "I read it somewhere."

"Where?" Jules asks. "Ye old book of children's rhymes? Sounds like a pilgrim wrote it."

"Maybe they did," says Cedrick. "They probably had vamps back then, too, huh, Mr. Rupert?"

"Tell me, Mr. Chambers," Mr. Rupert says as he ignores

Cedrick's question. "Have you ever been in a position to try using the rhymes? Maybe you could try a little experiment on your new bloodsucking best friend."

"We don't experiment on our friends," Jules says. "Why would you even say that?"

"Because you seem to enjoy spending time with him," Mr. Rupert says. "Might as well make it educational."

I look away from him. "Have *you* ever used the rhymes on a vampire?" I ask. "You're not a Vanquisher, so you probably only have the rhymes to defend yourself anyway, right?"

I glance back at him and he narrows his gaze at me. "I've seen a small child hold off a vampire with the rhymes. It's useful. It works. Remember that."

"Wait," I say. "You watched a kid use vampire rhymes against an actual vampire?" My mind goes in circles. "And you didn't help?"

"Of course I helped!" Mr. Rupert snaps. "My son was six at the time. Of course I—"

"You have a son?" Cedrick asks in shock.

Me and Jules stare at each other for a second. We're all a little surprised. Mr. Rupert is such a mean old man. I don't think any of us have really thought about his personal life and I know for a fact that none of us ever thought he might have kids.

"That's none of your business." Mr. Rupert shuffles some papers on his desk. "The less you know about me, the better. That way you'll never put me in danger with your reckless—"

"Daniel." My dad is suddenly standing at the bottom of the stairs. "Lesson over for today."

"No," Mr. Rupert says. "No. We've got more to cover."

"It wasn't a question," my dad says. He and Mr. Rupert exchange glances. "Come on," my dad says, gesturing to us. "I need some help in the garage."

Jules trips over their own legs as we scramble to get as far away from Mr. Rupert as fast as we can. Him opening up about his family seemed to have added gasoline to an already roaring fire of anger and I don't want to deal with it any longer than I have to.

We follow my dad into the garage and find that he's parked his car and my mom's car outside and that the garage doors are closed. My mom is standing in the middle of the empty parking spaces.

"What's going on?" I ask.

"We need some help," my mom says. "We have some old gear that I think we should take out of storage and inventory."

"Gear?" Cedrick asks. "Like, Vanquisher gear?" His voice is a whole octave higher when he's excited.

My mom smiles and gives him a wink. "Yes. But this is between us, got it? No one needs to know this stuff is here. Understood?"

I nod but as I look around the garage, I don't see anything except my dad's workbench, some of his tools, and the big green trash cans that go out to the curb on Fridays.

"Step back a little," my dad says. "Don't want y'all falling in."

Cedrick is scratching the top of his head, Jules looks confused, and I'm wondering if my parents have secret powers that let them see things other people can't see, because there is nothing interesting in our stank garage. My mom takes out something that looks like a garage door opener and presses a small gray button on the front. There's a low rumbling sound and the floor in the center of the garage slides open like horizontal elevator doors. A light flickers on from somewhere below.

"A secret room?" Cedrick asks. "No way!"

My dad chuckles and sets his hand on Cedrick's shoulder. I'm not laughing, though. Here's another secret. Something else I probably should have known about but here I am, learning of it for the first time.

"We're not supposed to have this stuff anymore," my mom says, like she can read my thoughts. "When we retired, it was meant to be for good. We were supposed to leave all this stuff behind."

I glance at her and her expression is an unreadable mask.

"What do you mean?" I ask. "Somebody told you that you had to leave whatever's down there behind? 'Lita told you that?" 'Lita was the leader of the Vanquishers at the time of the Reaping. She could have given that order but it doesn't make a lot of sense. 'Lita keeps her mask mounted above her bed but my mom couldn't hold on to her old Vanquisher stuff?

My mom shakes her head. "No. It's—it wasn't her."

Clearly, I'm missing something and my mom doesn't want to come out and say it so I wait but she doesn't offer anything else. Cedrick and Jules follow my dad down a short flight of stairs under the secret doors. I hang back, giving my mom another opportunity to be honest with me.

"Come on," my mom says. "We'll talk later. I promise."

She puts her arm around me and I know I'm not going to get anything else out of her right now so we follow everyone else into the room under the garage.

The stairway is tight and narrow but opens into a small space lined with metal shelves, each of them filled with neatly organized stacks of what looks like clothing. On the right side are crimson-red garments, the type of clothing Carmilla was known to have worn. There's a billowy red cape hanging from a hook and even a pair of sturdy red boots. On the left there are stacks of mismatched pants and shirts all neatly folded, tactical vests with a million pockets, and a tote full of gloves. And on the back wall are two masks hanging side by side—Carmilla's red cowl and face covering made of a thick fabric with spaces cut for the eyes and Threshold's mask, also red but made from something harder and resembling a hockey mask without all the little holes.

My mom runs her hands over the masks. "I don't think we'll need this but—"

"Samantha," my dad says. "There's no sense in trying to put on a brave face." My mom nods and he turns to us as Jules and

Cedrick both press their shoulders against mine. My dad sighs. "Listen, we have a strong suspicion that vampires are amassing some kind of force here in San Antonio. We don't know why. We don't know how it pertains to what happened to Aaron, but it's a real concern, so we're making sure we're prepared. We want you to be prepared, too."

My chest feels tight like it's being squeezed from the outside. My mom rummages around and pulls a big plastic container with a tight-fitting lid out from the bottom shelf and slides it over to us. Across the top are the letters "WC." I look at my mom.

"Wrecking Crew," my mom says. "Some extra gear. Thought maybe you'd like to try some on."

"Wait," Cedrick says. He shifts from one foot to the other, barely able to contain his excitement. "What's that mean?"

"Are we the Wrecking Crew now?" Jules asks.

My mom's expression is pinched. "I don't know if I'm comfortable with that."

"The Wrecking Crew fought the undead," I say.

"I don't need y'all to fight," my mom says. "I need you to keep yourselves safe. That's the priority."

"But the Wrecking Crew learned to fight so they could help you guys out," Jules says.

"They fought and sometimes they died," my mom says, her tone deadly serious. "Those of us who survived our time in the crew were lucky. Not everybody else was. We disbanded the Wrecking Crew in '98 specifically because of how dangerous it was. Vamps were targeting our junior members just to get at us."

"It was awful," my dad says.

"If it's too dangerous for us to be the new Wrecking Crew, why show us all this stuff?" I ask.

"Just like with a lot of other things right now, we're trying to figure out a new way of doing this," my mom says firmly. "We're trying to give you what you need to keep yourselves safe and you *are* the new Wrecking Crew even if it looks a little different for you than it did for us. As for other information you should know." She sighs. "Give me a little time to figure out how much to share. It's heavy, Boog. You have no idea."

At least she's acknowledging that there are definitely things she's keeping from me. I want her to tell me what it is but she seems set on keeping it to herself for now.

Cedrick pries open the lid of the container marked "WC" and inside are all kinds of outfits—pants with reinforced knees, boots in various sizes, jackets and vests with pockets and buckles, even a few plain cloth masks.

"Most of the clothing is reinforced," my mom says. "Everything is collared to protect the carotid arteries in the neck, the brachial arteries in the arms, and the femoral arteries in the legs. Those tend to be the places vamps go for first."

Cedrick snatches up a pair of cargo pants and clutches them

to his chest. "They're gonna go for my arteries? They wanna eat my arteries for a snack?"

Jules grins. "Forbidden Red Vines."

"And your dads make you eat all that healthy vegan stuff," I say. "Your blood probably tastes extra good to them."

We all giggle and so does my dad but a quick glance from my mom shuts down the fun.

"It's serious," she says. "I know y'all deal with stress by making jokes but it's not a game. Aaron is the exception to the rule and even then . . ." She trails off, her gaze drifting to the side. "Even then, you have to be careful. Go through this bin and find stuff that fits."

We nod and my mom climbs back up the stairs. My dad climbs up after her and me and Jules ro-sham-bo for a pair of thick black leggings with lots of little pockets and loops stitched in. I win, but we find an identical pair and decide our outfits will match. Near the bottom of the bin are a fitted black sweater and a pair of calf-high boots that look like they might fit me.

"The Vanquishers all have cool names," Cedrick says as he slips on a pair of black gloves. "We should have nicknames, too, right?"

"I don't think that's how it works," Jules says.

I nod. "Yeah. The Wrecking Crew takes over the Vanquisher names when it's their turn."

"Okay but we're switching things up now, right?" Cedrick

asks. "We should have names." He thinks for a minute. "I want y'all to call me Nosferatu Junior."

Jules almost looks angry. "I'm never ever gonna call you that."

"Me either," I say.

Cedrick looks disappointed. "Okay so no nicknames?"

"No," I say. "At least not right now."

"And it's never gonna be Nosferatu Junior," Jules says, ending the conversation right there.

Cedrick rolls his eyes and continues digging through the container of Wrecking Crew attire when above us, the side door on the garage creaks open and Mr. Rupert's exasperated breaths fill the air.

"Did you see the news?" he asks. "Just now. Did you see it?"

"No. What's happening?" my mom asks.

Mr. Rupert sighs. "Six people went missing last night. Six!"

I hear my mom inhale sharply.

"We cannot contain this, Samantha," Mr. Rupert says. "People will know what this means. They'll panic."

"It's not up to us," my dad says. "You know that. If it was, we'd tell everyone that they need to prepare, that they need to put the old protections back in place."

"Let's take this outside," my mom says. Her face appears at the top of the stairs. "I'll be right back." She disappears and I immediately pull Jules and Cedrick close to me.

"You hear that?" I ask, my heart thudding against my ribs. "Six people missing in one night."

"It's vampires," Cedrick says. "I know it."

I know he's right but I don't wanna say it. It feels bad, like something is creeping its way under my skin and wriggling around. It makes me shiver. "Did you hear what my dad said, though? About how it's not up to them to keep this a secret for much longer?"

"What does that mean?" Jules asks. "They're the Vanquishers. Don't they run this stuff? Isn't it all up to them?"

I shake my head. "That's what I thought, too, but not anymore. Those guys at my mom's job, those ones with the weird symbol on their coats, I think they have something to do with this. The way my mom was talking to them, it's almost like *they* were in charge."

Cedrick pulls on a black utility vest and is brainstorming what kind of things he's going to keep in his various pockets, none of which include weapons of any kind, when I hear my mom shriek from somewhere upstairs.

I bolt up the steps as Ced and Jules trail me out of the garage, down the hallway, and into the main house. In the living room, my mom has her hands cupped over her mouth, tears in her eyes. My dad is standing with his hand over his heart, in stunned silence. Mr. Rupert is there, so is 'Lita and Miss Celia. And there's someone else there, too. Someone I've never seen before—a tall man who looks like he's a little younger than my parents. He's got a fresh line-up and is dressed like he's about to go play basketball. He has a smile on his lips but he also looks a little sad.

"Casey?" my mom gasps through her fingers. "How did you—where—how?"

My dad puts his hand on the guy's shoulder and sighs. "I—I can't believe I'm seeing you again. Is this real?"

I clear my throat and everyone, including the stranger, turns to look at me.

'Lita smiles warmly. "Kids, come in here. I have someone I want you to meet." 'Lita, who is a full foot shorter than this guy, loops her arm around the man. "This is Casey. He's a former member of the Wrecking Crew."

CHAPTER 6

Another Vanquisher. Well, not technically a Vanquisher but still important. Nobody ever gives the Wrecking Crew a lot of thought. Everyone is focused on the main players but as Casey embraces everyone, I can see that he was—is—as important to them as they are to each other.

My mom calls Mr. Ethan and he arrives with Mr. Alex, both of them out of breath and in shock when they see Casey. 'Lita comes over and nudges me, Ced, and Jules over so we can shake Casey's hand and introduce ourselves one at a time.

"You guys have kids now," Casey says as he grins at us. "I can't believe it. I mean, I guess I can. It's great but a little weird."

"A lot has changed in the last twenty-something years," my dad says.

"You got that right," Casey says, running his hand over the top of his head.

"How are you here right now?" my mom asks. I think it comes out a little more blunt than she meant it to. "When we disbanded the Wrecking Crew, we told you all to scatter. We—we haven't seen you in so long. How did you even get here?"

Casey looks to 'Lita, who lowers herself onto the couch.

"I tried to keep watch from afar," 'Lita says, wringing her hands together in front of her. "It wasn't right that we had to sever ties the way we did. I always worried about Casey and the others. The way things ended—it wasn't right."

There it is again. That strange thing that's running under all of this. 'Lita would never knowingly do something she felt wasn't right. Again, it's like somebody was telling the Vanquishers what to do and it makes me wonder what kind of people even had the power to do that.

Casey walks over and squeezes 'Lita's hand.

"I didn't stop keeping watch until well after the Reaping," 'Lita says. "Casey is the only one I could pin down after all this time. The others scattered as we instructed them to. Left with their families and made lives for themselves away from San Antonio."

Casey looks down at the floor. "I never left. Never really felt like I could. The others had families to go back to."

'Lita's face is tight with emotion. Tears stand in her eyes. "I left money. Food. Whatever I thought you could use. But as time went on I saw you working, making a life, so I stepped back even further. I wanted you to have a chance at some kind of normalcy. In my own way I, too, became too complacent." She huffs. "Imagine that. The Mask of Red Death—letting her defenses down even a little."

"None of this is on you, Lidia," my mom says.

'Lita dabs at her eyes. "The past is a funny thing. You'd think it would stay there but it has a habit of coming back around again." She shakes her head. "Anyway, I thought we could use some extra help from someone we trust."

"It's good to have you back," Mr. Alex says to Casey.

I lean close to Jules. "We should leave them alone for a while."

They nod and we go upstairs while the adults continue their reunion.

In my room, I grab my laptop as Ced shuts the door.

"Cool, right?" he asks. "A member of the Wrecking Crew! Right here in your house!"

"It's cool," says Jules. "But do you know what kind of trouble we must be in to have to track down somebody like that and bring them back here?"

"We know things are bad but this makes it seem like things are about to go sideways," I say as I open my computer. I click around and open a few tabs.

"What are you doing?" Jules asks, sitting next to me and peering down at my screen.

"Earlier, I heard my mom say something about somebody named Mullins and somebody named Davis."

"Who the heck are they?" Ced asks as he takes up a seat on the other side of me.

"She was talking about those guys who were at her office. The guys in the black jackets." A Google search for the names turns up nothing useful at all.

"What about that symbol?" Cedrick asks. "Maybe we can find something about it?"

I make a better drawing of the symbol, snap a picture of it, and do a reverse image search. Some similar symbols pop up but nothing exact. I sit my computer on my nightstand and lie back across my bed.

"I don't know what to do," I say. "Feels like a dead end."

"An undead end," Cedrick chimes in.

"No more jokes from you, sir," Jules huffs.

My bedroom door suddenly bounces open and I sit bolt upright. Casey is standing in the doorway. He glances around and his gaze lands on my open laptop with the picture I'd taken of my drawing just sitting there. I snap it closed and he laughs.

"Sorry!" he says. "Your mom said the bathroom was up here."

"Across the hall," I say.

"The room with the toilet in it," Cedrick says.

Casey grins. "Right. Sorry." He goes out and closes the door behind him.

"You think he'll tell my mom what we were Googling?" I ask, suddenly concerned that this guy is gonna snitch.

"Nah," Jules says. "How would he even know what that is? Did Wrecking Crew members have all the same info as full-fledged Vanquishers?"

"I don't know," I say. "Maybe?" I listen for him to come out of the bathroom before I say anything else but he's taking his sweet time. "Let's ask if we can go out on the Green."

My mom says yes but only because she and everyone else have decided to move their get-together to the back porch, where they have a clear line of sight to the big expanse of green-space just outside the fence behind our house. We trudge out and sit in the grass under the bright afternoon sun. The day-light makes me feel safe but it also makes me feel far away from Aaron.

Jules plucks blades of grass out of the ground and tosses them at Ced. "What are we gonna do now?" they ask. "We don't know anything else about that symbol or those people at your mom's job. This is all just weird."

"And all these new missing people," Cedrick says. "It's creeping me out."

I'm about to tell Cedrick my theories when I spot Casey slipping through the back gate and heading our way.

"This man is lost again?" Cedrick asks. "I see why they cut him loose from the Wrecking Crew."

I stifle a laugh as Casey jogs up and plops down in the grass next to us.

"Ummmmmm, can we help you?" Cedrick asks, looking absolutely bewildered.

"Just wanted to say hi again," he says. "And sorry for just walking into your room. That was my mistake." He smiles and crosses his legs in front of him. "It's just wild seeing all of you. Your parents, they're legends. And now they have kids!" He slaps his knee and Jules jumps. "Weird!"

"Something's weird," Cedrick says under his breath. "And it sure ain't us."

Casey grins. "I'm not tryna be in your business but I couldn't help but notice something on your computer when I was upstairs."

My chest tightens up. "Okay?" I say, trying and failing to keep my cool.

"I was wondering if you know what it means?" he asks. "That symbol."

I don't know this dude at all and I'm still a little confused about how much members of the Wrecking Crew were in on when it came to Vanquisher stuff. If he doesn't know what the symbol means, he probably wasn't too involved, right?

"How old are you?" I ask.

Casey tilts his head and runs his hand over his mouth. "I'm forty. Why?"

"Because you're sitting over here with us like you're a big kid and it's weird," Cedrick says. "You're a stranger."

"I mean I'm not really a stranger," Casey says, still smiling. "I've known your parents since I was a kid."

"That's exactly the kind of thing a stranger would say,"

Cedrick says. "That's how they get you. They tell you they've known your parents forever and that it's totally fine but we're not falling for it, Casey."

Me and Jules and Casey just stare at Cedrick, who's all worked up now.

"Umm, okay," Casey says. "Sorry. I just—I just think it's so cool that you guys are the kids of the actual Vanquishers."

Cedrick is staring at this man like he wants to fight him. I pat Ced's shoulder and he sits back a little.

"So you were twenty when the Reaping happened?" I ask, doing the math in my head and trying to think of a way to calm the situation down.

"I wasn't at the Reaping," Casey says, glancing back toward my yard where everybody else is gathered on the back porch. "The Vanquishers disbanded the crew in 1998. I was sixteen when they cut me loose." He laughs a little.

"Cut you loose?" Jules asks. "Like, they fired you?"

Casey laughs and shakes his head. "No. Not like that. The Vanquishers were taking some heat for being in San Antonio. Carmilla had been killed the year before—"

"What?" Even though I can literally see my mom standing on the back porch, hearing that the Vanquisher she inherited her name from had been killed rocks me to my core.

Casey's shoulders move up and he grimaces. "I probably shouldn't have said it like that. Sorry. Listen, it's not my place to say any of this stuff. The Vanquishers dismantled the Wrecking

Crew and sent us home because they said things had become too dangerous. I didn't ask questions."

My mom and 'Lita are saying the same thing to us. "But you're asking questions now," I say. "About the symbol."

He stands up and brushes bits of grass off his shorts. "I've seen it before. Before the Reaping. Some guys showed up to one of our training camps. I don't know what was said, but everybody was pissed that they even knew where we were. I don't know what it means, but it's something I've thought about for a long time."

A thought pushes its way to the front of my mind but I don't come right out with it. If he takes it the wrong way, he might run back and tell my parents. I think for a minute, then decide it's worth the risk.

"So you weren't in on everything the Vanquishers knew?" I ask.

"No," Casey says. "That's not really how the crew operated."

"You think it's fair they kept things from you?" I ask.

Jules shoots me a what-the-heck-are-you-doing glance but I ignore it.

Casey sits back down and sighs. "Just between us? Not really. How can I keep myself safe if I don't have all the information? I was young, just a little older than you guys. I think I would have had an easier time if they'd been more open. Man, I wish I could be that young again. I'd have been a Vanquisher in no time." His head snaps up and he suddenly looks like he realizes he's said too much. "Look, I'm not talking bad about them. Sorry. Please don't say anything."

"We won't," I say. "I mean, maybe if you help us out with something, we won't say anything."

Casey's eyes grow wide. "Are you—are you blackmailing me?"

It's all eyes on me and Casey gives me a tight smile.

"No," I say even though that's exactly what I'm doing. "I'm just sayin'."

Casey looks to each one of us, then smiles. "What is it you need help with?" he asks.

"That symbol," I say. "The one I was looking at on my computer. Do you think you could help us look into it? You said you saw it before and I think it's connected to what's been going on lately. The disappearances, all that stuff."

Cedrick rolls his eyes and leans back in the grass. "Great. Tell him all our secrets. Now he's gonna snitch on us."

"No, I won't," Casey says, grinning. "I know what it's like to feel like you don't have all the information you need to really feel safe." His mouth is pinched as he says this, like he's stopping himself from saying more. "I'll see what I can find and I'll let y'all know. In the meantime, you don't say anything to your parents about what I said. Last thing I need is for them to be mad at me. We just got back in touch and I don't want to mess this up. Deal?"

I feel weird about asking for his help and even weirder about making a deal with him but I need to know what that symbol stands for and how it's connected to the new hive, the disappearances, the break-in at my mom's job, all of it.

"Deal," I say.

Casey nods. "It was good meeting all of you. I'll see y'all around." He gives us an awkward salute and strides back to the house.

"What's his deal?" Jules asks. "It's not giving creep vibes, but something is *off*, right? Like he wishes he was our age again or something."

"Definitely," I say. "You see how he's dressed?"

We all laugh and then Ced puts on his serious voice. "But do you think he's really gonna help us or is he gonna run back and tell our parents that we're being nosy?"

"I don't know," I say. "I guess we'll see."

CHAPTER 7

I sit on the couch in Aaron's living room as Jules and Cedrick play an overly aggressive game of Uno on the floor. We're killing time as we wait for Aaron to emerge. My mom and Miss Kim are in the basement when the doorbell rings. I'm on my feet but as soon as I step toward the door, my mom appears, shouldering her crossbow. She grasps it in one hand as Miss Kim appears from the basement and goes to the door. My mom nods at her and she opens the front door. Casey is on the stoop. Nobody says anything. He and my mom make eye contact and he steps over the threshold.

"We good?" he asks as he raises his hands in front of him.

My mom lowers the crossbow. "Yes. What are you doing here?" Her tone is clipped, and I can't help but wonder why. She'd been pretty happy to see Casey when he showed up the day before.

Miss Kim closes the door and it's only then that I see she's clutching a small beaker with a cork stuck in the top. Inside the glass container is a lime-green liquid.

"Ethan told me you were here," Casey says. He stands quietly for a minute and for some reason my heartbeat kicks up. Casey's fidgeting with the button on his jacket pocket. He's shifting his weight from one foot to the other.

"What's the problem, Casey?" my mom asks. "You look . . . nervous."

"I am," he says. "Old habits, I guess."

My mom steps toward him and there is something in the glances they exchange that chills me to the bone. There is something unspoken between them. My mom's finger has not moved from the trigger of her crossbow. "Casey. What is the problem?" My mom repeats the question with so much seriousness I feel like *I'm* in trouble.

"Ethan said you were here and he also said there's a vampire here," Casey says. "But both of those things can't be true at the same time, right? If you're here," he says to my mom, "any vamps in the vicinity would be vanquished."

I take a few steps toward the back door and Casey stares at me.

"And your kids are here?" he asks. "I'm confused."

My mom relaxes a little and rubs her temple. "How much did Ethan tell you?"

"He was in the process of saying more but I ran over here immediately," Casey says. "I had to see it for myself."

"*Him*," Miss Kim says. "Not 'it.' And my son isn't a specimen for you to examine."

"His name is Aaron," my mom says in her I'm-not-playin' voice. "And he is under our protection."

"A vampire is under the protection of the Vanquishers?" Casey asks. He looks genuinely confused.

"And the Wrecking Crew," Cedrick chimes in.

Casey's expression is a mix of surprise and confusion. By the way he narrows his eyes, there's a healthy dose of anger in there, too.

"You re-formed the Wrecking Crew?" Casey asks. "With your kids?"

My mom shakes her head. "It's not what it sounds like. Things have changed." She's not explaining herself to Casey. She's just stating facts.

"And the vampire?" Casey asks.

"He's our friend." Cedrick is wearing the tactical vest he took from the bin in my garage and he runs his hand over one of the pockets that is meant to hold a stake but, in Cedrick's case, is secreting a Capri Sun.

Casey pulls out a chair and sits down at the table. "Things *have* changed." He's quiet for a moment, and when he speaks again his entire demeanor has changed. His voice is light, he smiles, his shoulders relax a little. "I'm not judging," he says. "I'm just curious, you know?" He grins, which seems to disarm Miss Kim a little but I don't buy it. Jules is right. Something is up with him.

Miss Kim sits at the dining room table and puts the beaker of green liquid down.

"What's that?" Jules asks.

Miss Kim smiles. "That's for Aaron. I've been working day and night and I think I'm onto something here."

"A cure?" I ask as Cedrick and Jules join me at the table.

Casey's head whips around. "You're trying to cure him?"

Miss Kim nods. "Yes. But I'm nowhere close. The best I can do is this." She taps the beaker with her finger and the green liquid sloshes up on the side. "I've been working with some different compounds, trying to isolate the cause of the vampirism on a cellular level, but it's unlike anything I've ever seen. It changes so rapidly. It adapts. I'm worried some of the changes are irreversible." Her bottom lip quivers a little and she sighs. I put my hand on hers. "So I shifted my focus," she continues. "Tried to find something that could help him feel more normal even if he's changed. This is like sunscreen except you drink it. It lets him walk in the daylight for about an hour per dose. It's not much but it's something."

"So Aaron can come out in the daytime now?" I ask excitedly. I thought we were gonna have to wait years for Aaron to build up a tolerance to the sun. I'd learned in the book we borrowed from Cedrick's dads that older vamps can and do spend at least some of their time in the daylight hours and in the volume I have in my room, the Vanquishers talk about how the older vamps could walk in the daylight, which made their jobs that much harder.

"That's still probably not a great idea at this moment," my mom says. "Not with everything going on, but eventually, yes. He can come out more often and I think that'll be good for him. He needs his family and his friends." She smiles at Miss Kim.

"So where is he?" Casey asks. "I'd like to meet him."

Miss Kim's mouth flattens into a tight line and I suddenly feel even more protective of my friend than I already do.

"He'll be here shortly," my mom says.

"We'll ask him if he even wants to meet you," Cedrick says.

Casey looks at Ced and blinks repeatedly. "Um. Okay."

Cedrick doesn't look away and an awkward silence envelops the room. It's broken a few moments later by a gentle tapping at the back door. Miss Kim hops up and unlocks the door, allowing Aaron inside.

Casey rises out of his chair like he's being pulled up by a string. The look on his face is a mix of curiosity, fear, and bewilderment. I immediately move to Aaron's side and slip my arm under his. He squeezes my hand.

"How'd you sleep?" I ask.

"Like the dead," Aaron says, grinning, his little eyeteeth poking out from under his lip.

"We brought Uno," Jules says. "Cedrick wants to play but he cheats."

"You can't cheat at Uno," Cedrick says as he slaps palms with Aaron and hands him a rolled-up comic he had stashed in one of his vest pockets. "House rules are anything goes."

Casey is still staring at Aaron, who stares back. Casey's hand moves to his pocket, but my mom catches his wrist before he even knows what's happening.

"Please tell me you don't have a weapon on you," my mom says.

Casey is silent but he lowers his eyes.

My mom pats the jacket pocket and her mouth turns down. "Give it to me, right now."

Casey's gaze traces from the floor to the ceiling. From his jacket pocket he produces a small orb about the size of a walnut. Its outside coating is so black that as Casey hands it to my mom, it looks like there is a hole in her palm.

"Why would you bring this here?" my mom asks in a whisper.

Casey's face is drawn tight. "I was afraid."

"Of me?" Aaron asks in a way that breaks my heart. He doesn't want anybody to be afraid of him.

"What even is that?" Cedrick asks.

My mom sets the orb on the table and again I can't get over how dark it is. It's blacker than any shade of dark I've ever seen.

"It's a Vanta-black orb," my mom says. "It's one of Miss Celia's inventions. It was the weapon of choice for Dayside."

We all crowd the table to get a better look but Aaron hangs back.

"Don't touch it," my mom warns. "It's a casing made of

carbon fiber and infused with a substance known as Vanta-black—Vertically Aligned Nano Tube Array Black."

"What did you just say?" Cedrick asks. "It sounds like a spell."

My mom narrows her eyes at Casey. "It's not a spell, it's science. Its outer coating is the darkest shade known to science. It absorbs 99.9 percent of all visible light so wherever it is looks like a void."

"Is there something inside it?" I ask.

My mom stares at the orb. "Daylight," she whispers.

Aaron takes another step back and Miss Kim moves in front of him.

"How do you get daylight inside of it?" Jules asks.

"It's a chemical process," my mom says as she picks up the orb again. "There's a button. When you press it, it opens and the chemicals inside mix with the carbon and oxygen in the air. They create a burst of UV light as bright as the sun. It has a devastating effect on the undead and can cause temporary blindness in the living." She turns back to Casey. "Where did you get this?"

"I've had it this whole time," he says. "Ever since you all . . . retired." He takes a beat, then continues. "Just in case, you know? I took it from the armory when you guys shut the Wrecking Crew down. I didn't want to be out here unarmed."

"Were you gonna use that on me?" Aaron asks.

Casey jumps at the sound of Aaron's voice, like he'd

forgotten he was even there. "Sorry, kid. Really. I was just—you don't understand. I was with the Vanquishers. They taught me to fight the undead. It was kind of our job. I heard there was a vamp here so I thought . . ." He looks at the orb. "I don't know. I wanted to be prepared."

"Aaron is twelve," Miss Kim says. "He's a child."

"And a vampire turned him," my mom says. "That is against one of their founding tenets. They don't do that."

"Looks like they did," Casey says. He sticks out his hand to Aaron. "I'm sorry, Aaron. I didn't mean to scare you."

Aaron steps forward and shakes Casey's hand but as he does, he lets his jaw unhinge a little. It makes his face look long, the skin stretched too thin over his temples. He lets his eyes go black as dark veins snake up from under the collar of his shirt and crawl under the skin of his neck and face. "You didn't," Aaron says. "Don't even worry about it."

Casey stumbles back and sits down hard in his chair. I turn to Aaron, my heart thudding in my chest. I quickly mask the fear with a smile but I feel awful that there is some part of me that is scared of Aaron. I shake off those thoughts.

"Do you have any other stolen weapons I need to know about?" my mom asks.

"No, ma'am," Casey says.

"Do you mind if I take a look?" Miss Kim asks, shooting Casey a dagger of a glance. "It's fascinating tech. Y'all still making these?"

"Not in a while," my mom says. "Come on. I'll walk it downstairs for you." She turns to Casey, eyeing him carefully. Something silent passes between them and my mom and Miss Kim disappear into the basement.

"If you try anything funny, Aaron will snap your back off," Cedrick says as he sits down at the table.

"What's that even mean?" Casey asks, watching Aaron carefully.

Cedrick makes some weird moves with his hands like he's breaking something in half and throwing it on the floor. "Just like I said. Snap your back right off."

Aaron chuckles as he opens the fridge and grabs his Hydro Flask. He gulps the liquid down and then lowers himself into the chair directly next to Casey. "I'm not snapping anything. At least not right now." He doesn't look at Casey but we all know who he's talking to.

I sit down and rest my elbows on the table. Lowering my voice, I lean toward Casey. "Find out anything about that symbol?"

Casey is still staring at Aaron but this question seems to snap him out of his trance. "Uh, oh, right. Yeah actually. I did."

Jules and Cedrick lean in close. Aaron stays completely still.

"I found a facility on the east side of town that used to be a shipping warehouse in the sixties. Then it got sold to someone else and ever since then people who live or work over there have been reporting strange activity—lots of unmarked cars, major security precautions, and this—" He pulls out his phone, taps around on the screen, and then turns the phone toward us.

It's a photo of two men in black jackets, the strange symbol clearly visible, going into the big gray warehouse.

"Where'd you get that?" I ask.

"Reddit," Casey says.

"That's why we can't find anything about that symbol," Jules says. "Reddit is probably one of the sites our parents have blocked."

"Not surprised," Casey says. "Y'all don't need to be on there."

"So, what's the facility for?" I ask.

"I don't know," Casey says. "I'm gonna go check it out, though. See what I can find."

"We're going, too," I say.

"Absolutely not," Casey says. "I don't know what it is or who's behind it, but if it has anything to do with vamps, it's way too dangerous."

"Oh come on!" I say a little too loudly. "We've been out after the streetlights go on. We're not little kids."

Casey bites back a laugh. "Uh, you are little kids. That's literally exactly what you are." He gets up and straightens out his sweater. "I'm heading out. Tell your mom I said bye and that I'll see her tomorrow."

He leaves without another word and Aaron goes to the door to lock it.

"You think he's going to that warehouse right now?" Cedrick asks.

Aaron suddenly disappears in a cloud of black smoke, then reappears a few seconds later. "Casey's driving a black car with a white stripe down the middle. License plate KLF-2740."

"How do you know that?" I ask.

"I went to look," Aaron says. "I can see really well in the dark. I got up on the roof and watched him drive off. He's heading toward downtown."

"Everybody upstairs," Cedrick says. "Right now."

He runs up the stairs before explaining himself and we all rush up after him. Aaron just appears in his room with wispy tendrils of curling black smoke encircling him. We close the door and huddle up.

"You gotta follow him," Cedrick says, looking at Aaron and then at me.

"What?" I ask. "No. I can't. My mom will kill me. You remember what happened last time we snuck out." Our outing to the park to meet Aaron after he'd been bitten was a disaster. Our parents found out and came to get us. Being on punishment like that isn't something I want to have to deal with, especially not right now.

Cedrick lowers his voice. "Aaron's got all kinds of new powers. He can help you sneak out."

Aaron leans in close. "I know I'm a vampire now, but I feel like my mom would find a way to make me human again just so she could kill me if I sneak out of here."

"You can literally fly," Cedrick says. "You can turn into a shadow. You're made for sneaking around."

Jules crosses their arms. "What do you want them to sneak out for?"

"Go follow Casey because I can almost guarantee he's headed to that place on the east side to check out that symbol and we need to know what's up with that." He turns to me. "Me and Jules will stay. We'll cover for you. Go with Aaron and get back here ASAP."

Aaron shakes his head. "I don't even know if these new abilities can help me hide Boog in the dark or if we can travel together."

"Didn't you pick Boog up and carry her to the end of the street when those other vamps were after you?" Jules asks.

Aaron and I exchange glances.

"I guess," Aaron says. "And maybe . . ." He lifts his hand and as he reaches toward me, his arm dissolves into a cloud of wispy black smoke. "Just hold still, okay, Boog?"

I nod but my heart is pounding against my ribs so hard it feels like it's trying to escape. The black smoke encircles my arm all the way up to my shoulder. It's icy cold and the feel of it makes goose bumps erupt on my skin. My arm is nearly invisible.

"Okay so you know that works," Cedrick says. "And Boog, you're the one who saw the symbol *and* the guys who were wearing it so it's gotta be you."

I'm still peering down at my arm when the door creaks open. Aaron's arm re-forms from the smoke as my mom steps into the room.

"Where'd Casey go?" she asks.

"He said he had to take off," I say. "He wanted me to tell you he'd see you tomorrow."

My mom looks puzzled. "Oh, okay. What are y'all plotting in here?"

"World domination," Jules says, grinning.

"I wouldn't even be surprised at this point," she says. "Listen, me and Miss Kim are working in the basement. Are y'all good to hang out for a while?"

"We're good," I say, knowing that we're about to break a bunch of rules and that if we get caught, I might never see the light of day again.

"Be good," my mom says, closing the door behind her.

When we're sure she's in the basement, Cedrick goes to the window and opens it. Aaron looks at me like he's trying to figure out the best way to do this.

"So, I think if I cloak you and then hold really tight to your arm, we should be okay," Aaron says. "Just don't look down and don't let go."

I have so many doubts and I'm about to say every single one of them out loud when a dark cloud envelops my entire body. I feel like I've been dropped into an ice-cold bath. The rush of frigid air snatches my breath away. There's a rush of wind. I shut my eyes tight. Aaron's hand is there somewhere in the dark, holding fast to my wrist, and I hear his voice close to my ear.

"Hang on, Boog."

Suddenly, we're moving. My feet aren't on the floor. I don't open my eyes because I'm terrified of what I'll see. Then just as suddenly, my feet are planted firmly on a hard surface. The cold around me is gone and the warm muggy air of late spring fills my lungs. I open my eyes to find myself standing on the top of the Cold Stone in the strip mall on the other side of the Green. Aaron is standing next to me. My stomach heaves and I throw up.

CHAPTER 8

"You okay?" Aaron asks.

"No," I say as I try to clean myself up a little. I wipe my mouth with the back of my hands and try to breathe. "What—what just happened?"

"I was gonna take off toward the east side of town but I don't really know where we're going," says Aaron.

The parking lot of the strip mall is empty and the pet supply shop where Mrs. Lambert gets the food for her lizards has a sign hanging in the front window that now says Out of Business.

"Right," I say as I gather myself and try not to puke on Aaron's shoes. "We should follow Casey's car. Did you see it?"

"I saw which way he went," Aaron says. "I can go see if I can get eyes on him. You ready to go back up?"

I'm not but we're here and the only other option is going home and waiting for those guys with the symbol on their jackets to show themselves again. I take a deep breath, give Aaron a nod, then shut my eyes tight. I'm surrounded by dark and cold again, the feeling of the ground moving from under my feet. A rush of air. This time it lasts for what feels like forever and when the ground is firmly under me again, I open my eyes to find that we're standing on top of a warehouse in a part of the city I don't recognize.

I sink to my knees. "Don't puke. Don't puke. Don't puke."

Aaron is at my side, with his hand on my back.

"How much further do we have to go?" I ask. "I don't think I can keep going like this."

"I think we're already here," he says quietly.

I glance up and, in the darkness directly across from us, is a large gray warehouse surrounded by a high fence with barbed wire running along the top of it. Spotlights illuminate the driveway as a truck waits for the gate to open in front of it. Someone in a uniform comes out of a small guardhouse, speaks to the driver, then returns to his station as the gate rolls open and the truck passes through.

Aaron scoots closer to me and slings his arm around my shoulders. Our bodies are instantly obscured by a swirling black mist. We watch in silence as a car turns onto the street, its headlights beaming. As it gets closer I can see that it's a black sports car with a white stripe right down the middle.

"That's Casey's car," I say.

I expect him to zoom by. He made it seem like he'd just found out about this place and I can't imagine him just waltzing up to the gate.

"He's just gonna go in?" Aaron asks.

I reach for my phone so that I can take some pictures but realize I've left it at Aaron's house. It's probably for the best because my location's on and the last thing I need is for my mom to see that I'm on the other side of town and not in Aaron's room.

Casey's car sits in front of the gate but it doesn't open for him like it did for the truck. A man comes out of the guardhouse, leans down to the window, then takes a walkie-talkie from its holster on his belt and speaks into it. I can't hear what he's saying but a minute later, two men approach the gate from the inside.

Casey exits the car and Aaron and I duck down, lying on our bellies on the rooftop. We're still cloaked by the black smokelike mist Aaron can produce and it's so cold I have to clench my jaw tight to keep my teeth from chattering together.

Even at a distance, I recognize the men on the other side of the gate. They're the same people who had been questioning my mom at her job after the break-in—the men she'd called Mullins and Davis.

"I wish I could hear what they're saying," I whisper.

Aaron nods. Even if we can't hear them, it's clear that Casey and the men know each other. Casey gestures with his hands and points at the large gray warehouse behind the gate. It's only then that I see the same symbol from the men's jackets emblazoned in black on the side of the building.

The man with the dark hair—I don't know if he's Mullins or Davis—sticks his finger in Casey's face, then crosses his arms over his chest. The other man points to Casey's car. Casey flinches at the men, like if there wasn't a gate between them he'd be ready to fight. Then he turns and stomps back to his car, gets in, and tears out of the driveway, tires screeching.

"What the heck is that about?" I ask. "He knows these dudes?" I can't think straight. "We gotta get back so we can tell Ced and Jules."

Aaron nods. "You ready?"

I nod and Aaron grabs hold of my arm and suddenly I'm leaving the ground and my stomach is turning over.

Somebody who was driving along Loop 1604, probably somewhere around the H-E-B on Blanco Road, definitely got a windshield full of puke courtesy of me being unable to hold it in until my feet were safely back on the ground.

We land in Aaron's backyard and instead of the soft touchdown we'd made on the roof of the warehouse, our landing in the yard feels like falling out of the sky. I hit the ground hard, knocking the wind right out of my chest. Aaron tumbles down next to me, the billowing black smoke is gone, and he rolls up to a sitting position, clutching his arm.

I gasp and cough as I try to force the air back into my lungs. I peer up at Aaron's bedroom window as Cedrick leans out of it, his eyes wide, his mouth twisted in a grimace.

"Your mom's coming!" he scream-whispers into the dark. "Get in here! Now!"

I stumble to my feet and before I can blink, Aaron's at my side, scooping me up and dropping me in the middle of his room, where I lie sprawled on my back, my arms and legs stuck out like a starfish. My mom opens the bedroom door and pokes her head in.

Jules is sitting on the floor staring at me. Cedrick is by the open window and Aaron has appeared at his desk, legs crossed, comic book in hand.

"What, uh, what are you doing?" my mom asks.

Jules shrugs. "Being weird."

My mom puckers her lips. "At least you're honest." She looks at me again and I grin through the pain that's blooming in my tailbone. "I thought I heard a noise," she says. "Cedrick, close that window and lock it."

"Yes, ma'am," Cedrick says.

My mom looks us over again. "Just a few more minutes and then we can head home."

"Okay," I say, holding my breath.

She backs out and closes the door behind her. I don't move

until her footsteps have disappeared down the stairs. As soon as she's out of earshot I groan and roll onto my side. Jules is there, helping me sit up, and Aaron is scooting a small trash can toward me with his foot.

"What is happening?" Cedrick asks. "Y'all disappeared!"

"We followed Casey," I say as I try to steady myself. "I got sick."

"So he can carry you?" Jules asks. "It works?"

"It works," Aaron says. "I gotta be careful, though, because it feels like I'm not really holding on to anything. I guess I'm stronger than I was before." He smiles but not a second later his mouth turns down and he winces, grabbing his arm.

I'm on my feet, pushing aside the sick feeling in my stomach. I grab Aaron's arm and push his sleeve up. Tracing down his forearm is a nasty cut. Little tendrils of black snake off the edges of the wound.

"Oh no," I say. "Does your mom have a first aid kit? We gotta cover this up. It might get—" I stop because Aaron is staring at me. Smiling. "Why are you smiling?" I ask. "This is serious."

Aaron glances down at his wound. I follow his gaze and right before my eyes, the injury seals itself up. The smooth brown skin of his arm looks like he'd never been injured at all.

"Oh man," Jules says. "You can just heal up like that?"

Aaron nods.

"What happened anyway?" Cedrick asks.

"I caught my arm on one of the tree branches outside."

"The holly trees," I say quietly. I can't imagine what a stake made from one of those trees might do to a vamp. "We gotta be more careful. The protections our parents put up are to protect us from the bad vampires but they'll hurt you, too."

I squeeze Aaron's arm.

"Let's tell them what we saw," Aaron says.

I tell Jules and Cedrick about Casey pulling up to the strange warehouse and how he seemed to know the same two people my mom had spoken to. We're all in agreement that it's weird and makes us all suspicious of Casey.

"Feels like he's trying to stick his nose where it doesn't belong," Cedrick says. "I've had a bad feeling about him from the jump."

Jules nods. "Boog, your mom's not telling us everything and we're the official Wrecking Crew now. Casey was in the Wrecking Crew back in the day, so she's probably not telling him anything new either, right?"

I nod. "Yeah. I think she has some doubts about him, too. You saw her face when he showed up here? She's annoyed."

"Hold on," Aaron asks. "You're the Wrecking Crew now?"

"We need to do a better job of keeping you caught up on stuff that happens in the daylight hours," I say. "But yeah. *We're* the Wrecking Crew now. You're part of it, too."

Aaron smiles and we all huddle in close.

"We stick together," I say. "Nobody gets left behind and we don't keep secrets from each other. Deal?"

"Why are you talking like we're about to go off to war?" Cedrick asks.

Jules narrows their eyes. "Things are getting serious, Ced. More people missing, Casey's suspect, Mr. Rupert has lost his entire mind, Aaron's a vampire but we still don't know who bit him, and our parents are hiding something about these people with the symbol on their coats."

"You're forgetting the most important thing," Cedrick says.

I turn to him. "What's that?"

Cedrick's mouth turns down. "In the middle of all this stuff, we still gotta do homework."

The next day after school, Mr. Rupert is going on and on about Vanquisher history and I feel like my head is going to explode. He's gone over most of this stuff already. I have it memorized. I want something new, something we haven't talked about before.

I raise my hand and Mr. Rupert nods at me.

"Were there other groups of Vanquishers?" I ask. "Everything you've told us so far is about our parents or the Vanquishers that came before them but they were all right here. What about in other places?"

Mr. Rupert smiles and it's weird. "It's a very good question,

Miss Wilson. Yes. There were other groups of slayers around the world." Mr. Rupert points at a large map he's taped across the whiteboard in my basement. "Each region had its own set of Vanquishers, though they went by other names."

"What happened to them?" I ask. "Are they still around?"

"I honestly don't know," Mr. Rupert says. "There had been some communication between groups in the past, maybe three or four generations ago, but not now, as far as I'm aware."

"The Reaping was only twenty years ago," I say. "Why did the Vanquishers last so long here?"

Mr. Rupert is smiling again, and Cedrick makes a noise like he's stifling a laugh. "The Vanquishers endured here in the States because of a perfect storm of terrible circumstances," Mr. Rupert says. "Global populations of vampires were already dwindling and those that remained flocked to this place. This so-called land of opportunity was exactly that for the undead. A disposable population of stolen and displaced people to feed off of." Mr. Rupert pauses, takes a wavering breath, and continues. "Vampires had the ability to use their power indiscriminately in this place and it became one of their strongest footholds. This was a vampire's paradise. The Vanquishers formed and then, in about 1860, they created the Wrecking Crew to recruit and train people who would take over their mantles and become Vanquishers themselves one day. Usually people who had been left alone because of the actions of vampires or people who had close ties to the Vanquishers themselves."

Cedrick groans and Mr. Rupert frowns at him.

"Am I boring you, Mr. Chambers?" Mr. Rupert asks.

"Yes," Cedrick says. "You are. I can't take it."

Mr. Rupert is about to go off on him but I raise my hand again and ask my question before he has a chance to say anything else.

"I want to know about the Wrecking Crew," I say. "Like, did the Vanquishers share everything they knew with the crew? What was that like for them?"

"Would this have anything to do with the reappearance of Casey?" Mr. Rupert asks.

Cedrick and Jules sit up in their chairs.

"Yes," I say honestly. "He's back but he seems a little . . . off."

"How so?" Mr. Rupert asks.

I lean my elbows on the desk. "I don't know. I just think it's weird. I know 'Lita got in touch with him because all this stuff is happening and she thinks we need some more help but—"

"All of that is beyond your concern," Mr. Rupert says. "But regarding your earlier question, no. The members of the Wrecking Crew were not privy to everything the Vanquishers knew. That was done for their own safety. Many of the Wrecking Crew members were children when they were brought on. When junior members graduated to being full-fledged Vanquishers, that is when the most secret of information was passed to them."

I quickly pull out a piece of paper and draw the symbol I'd

seen on the men's jackets and on the warehouse. "Do you know what this is?"

Mr. Rupert looks at the drawing and as someone who wore every little bit of anger or frustration on his face, his expression doesn't change.

"No," he says. "What is it?"

"Never mind," I say, crumpling up the paper.

"So when me, Boog, Jules, and Aaron become Vanquishers, we'll get to know all the secrets, too?" Cedrick asks.

I don't know if that's even something I want but it'd be nice to know what those people with the weird symbol want and why they're harassing my mom.

Mr. Rupert's face twists up. "What do you mean 'and Aaron'?"

"We're the Wrecking Crew now," Cedrick says. "So when we're Vanquishers—"

Mr. Rupert slams his hand down on the desk and we all jump.

"Aaron will never be a Vanquisher," Mr. Rupert says. "Bloodsucking monsters don't get to have that honor."

A bolt of anger courses straight through me. "He's not a monster."

"You keep saying that, Miss Wilson," Mr. Rupert says quietly. "Who are you trying to convince? Me or yourself?"

"You don't know him!" I shout. I've never yelled at a teacher. Ever. But I can't sit here and let him talk about Aaron like this. "What is your problem? What did he ever do to you?"

"What those monsters have done to me is beyond anything you could ever imagine, Miss Wilson," Mr. Rupert says as he reels in his anger. "You're dismissed." He turns his back to us and I don't wait for him to say anything else. I grab my stuff and walk straight upstairs.

Cedrick and Jules meet me in the living room and a few moments later, Mr. Rupert emerges from the basement and walks out the front door. Cedrick goes and locks it behind him.

"I'm not letting him back in," he says. "He can stay out there when it gets dark, too. Maybe a vamp will have him as a snack."

"Not okay, Cedrick," Mr. Alex says from our kitchen. "We're not wishing that on anybody."

Cedrick hangs his head as he plops down on the couch next to me. My parents are at work and Mr. Alex is hanging out with us until we all meet up for our nightly check-in. We do our homework, talk trash about Mr. Rupert, and then watch movies until just before sunset.

My parents arrive home looking exhausted and they sit at the table as everyone else begins to pile in. Miss Celia and 'Lita come over, followed by Mr. Ethan and Casey.

The sun is still burning orange in the sky when the doorbell rings and Mom goes to answer it. It's Aaron and Miss Kim. Casey leans toward the window where the sky is still bright, then snaps his gaze back to Aaron.

"How are you outside right now?" Casey asks.

Miss Kim ushers Aaron inside and produces her little beaker of green liquid. "Works pretty good, right?"

My mom smiles but Casey just looks stoic. The adults all gather around the dining room table as Aaron comes into the living room and sits down on the carpet in front of me. He has a bag slung over his shoulder.

"What's in there?" I ask.

He pats the bag as he sits it on the floor. "Snacks."

We share a knowing little glance. He's got O negative Capri Suns in there. I just know it.

"Y'all are not gonna believe what I found out I can do," he says. "Cedrick, remember when you were telling me it'd be cool if I could turn into a wolf?"

Cedrick scoots to the edge of the couch. "Don't play with me right now. Please tell me you learned how to do it. Please!"

"Not that," Aaron says. "But something else. Look."

He raises his arm and it turns to black wispy smoke. Then, it solidifies into a small black shape. Two red eyes peer out, wings sprout, and suddenly I'm looking at a leathery vampire bat.

"What?!" Cedrick yelps. "No way!"

Mr. Ethan stands up, his hand on his waistband where his length of silver-infused coiled rope hangs.

"Dad, it's fine," Cedrick says. "Look! Aaron can turn parts of himself into a bat!"

Mr. Ethan sits back down but Casey comes over and watches Aaron intently.

"That's amazing," Casey says.

I stand and grab Aaron by the arm and pull him toward

my room. Jules scoops up his bag and follows us up with Cedrick at our heels. We go in my room and close the door.

"We just left Casey hanging down there," Jules says.

"I know," I say. "Because I don't want him getting close to Aaron. We don't know enough about him yet. I don't know if y'all caught it, but Mr. Rupert thought it was a little weird that Casey's here now."

"He said that?" Aaron asks.

"No but I could tell. When I brought it up he wasn't happy," I say.

Aaron still has his bat floating in the air next to him.

"How are you doing that?" Jules asks.

Aaron shrugs. "I just kept thinking about what Cedrick said. The wolf thing. I heard stories that vampires could turn themselves into other stuff—mist, shadows, and bats. I knew I could do the first two, but bats?" He holds his hand up and the bat sits in his palm, then dissolves into a hazy smoke that rejoins with Aaron's body. "I just tried it. I don't really know how. I just kind of thought about it and then it happened."

Aaron's face suddenly shifts, elongates a little. There's a popping noise at his temples and he grasps his hands together in front of him, his head bowed. Cedrick moves back. Jules is frozen where they are and so am I.

"It takes a lot out of me," Aaron says. "Can you hand me my bag?"

Jules reaches out with trembling hands, picks up Aaron's

bag, and passes it to me. I don't look Aaron in the face as I unzip it. Inside is an insulated lunch box and when I open it there are two thermoses that are warm to the touch. I hand one to Aaron. He flips the lid up and drains the entire thing in one long gulp. When I finally look at him, his face has settled into its regular position, and he looks like himself again.

I take a deep breath but the relief only lasts a second. Suddenly, Aaron is on his feet. His eyes are swimming with red and his face is elongated again.

"Do you—do you need more?" I ask, fumbling with the bag to try and get the other thermos out.

"No," Aaron snaps. His voice is otherworldly, like something I've never heard.

Cedrick and Jules jump up and stumble into the corner by the door.

I slowly stand up, my hands out in front of me. "Aaron?" I ask gently. "Hey, Aaron. You okay? What do you need? What's wrong? Here." I hold out the other thermos to him but my hands are trembling so bad I drop it and it rolls across the floor. Aaron doesn't even glance at it.

Aaron ascends into the air like he's being lifted by an invisible string. His breathing is ragged. He hovers a foot off the floor. I search for his face in the swirling mist that has begun to engulf his body and when I find it, I scream. I can't help it.

Red flecks glint in his solid black eyes. His eyeteeth are

protruding from under his top lip. His jaw unhinges and drops down making his mouth a gaping black cave. His fingers elongate into pointed claws. Jules whimpers from behind me and Cedrick grabs tight to them.

"Boog," Aaron says in that voice that sounds like a terrible, monstrous echo. "Hide."

CHAPTER 9

There is an avalanche of footsteps on the stairs. The door to my room bounces open violently and my mom steps in, crossbow at her side, her eyes wide. She raises it just slightly as she puts her focus on Aaron.

"How many?" she asks him. The tone in her voice makes me freeze. She's scared.

"How many what?" I ask. But she's not looking at me at all.

Aaron lowers his gaze and it terrifies me, but my mom steps closer to him. "Aaron, baby, I know it's hard but try to concentrate. You gotta focus right now. Our lives depend on it."

"Mom, you're scaring me," I say. "What's—"

She shushes me and keeps her gaze locked on Aaron.

"How many?" she asks again.

"Five," Aaron says. "I think."

My mom nods. "Are you in control right now? Remember what we talked about. You are in control, Aaron. You have a choice, baby." Aaron nods and my mom finally looks at me. "Vampires. On the perimeter. Get to the basement. Now."

I grab Jules and Cedrick and run into the hallway and down the stairs. I'm headed to the basement but as I pass by the living room, Mr. Alex yells.

"I'm staying with you," he says to Mr. Ethan.

"No," Mr. Ethan says as he uncoils a length of shimmering rope and loops it around his hand. "And you know why you can't. Take the kids. Keep them safe."

Mr. Alex kisses Mr. Ethan, then runs to my side and grabs Cedrick by the arm.

"Dad?" Cedrick asks, looking up at Mr. Alex.

"Come on," Mr. Alex says. He pulls us toward the basement steps.

I glance back and see my mom staring at me as her crossbow sits ready at her shoulder. Tears well up in my eyes. She rushes to me and pulls me to her chest.

"Nothing to cry for, baby," she says even though her eyes are glassy, too. "Take this."

She sets the small pitch-black orb she'd found on Casey in my palm.

"If they get in, if they get near you, push the button and then close your eyes. Make sure Aaron isn't around when it goes off. Understand?"

"Mom, I—"

"Malika," my mom says. "Do you understand me?"

"Yes," I say as I slip the orb into my pocket.

She pushes me toward the basement steps where Mr. Alex is waiting. He pulls me down as a calamitous thud rocks the house.

I join Jules and Cedrick in the basement and we quickly crowd into the pantry where the large container of garlic bulbs is stashed. When we're all inside, Mr. Alex grabs a bunch of the bulbs and throws them down on the ground, smashing them into smelly little slicks at the base of the door. The pungent odor fills the room. It makes my eyes water. There is shouting from overhead, pounding footsteps.

"Dad," Cedrick says. "What is going on?"

Mr. Alex pulls us all close to him, his back against the closed pantry door.

"I—I'm not sure," he stammers. "Boog, your mom got one of her feelings. She knew something was up. This shouldn't be happening. We've fortified everything."

"Aaron said there were five vampires out there," I say.

The color drains away from Mr. Alex's face. "Oh no," he says, his voice barely a whisper.

Jules fights back tears. "Are we gonna be safe?" they ask.

Mr. Alex's breaths come in quick puffs as the banging and shouting from upstairs gets louder.

"Listen to me," he says. "If you see an opportunity to run, take it. If something happens to me, leave. Go to Miss Kim's."

"What?" Cedrick asks. "No. Dad. I'm not—"

"Cedrick Anthony Chambers, do not test me," Mr. Alex says as tears fill his eyes. "Do as I say. I love you. All of you. Go to Miss Kim's. Got it?"

I begin to sob. It pours out of me. I've never been this scared in my whole life. I lean against Mr. Alex and he's shaking but so am I so it doesn't matter. I hold Jules's hand so tight I worry I'm hurting them, but they're just staring at the ceiling.

"I think I heard 'Lita," they say.

I listen closely. They're right. I hear 'Lita shouting something over and over again but I can't make it out. I hope it's orders. I hope her telling everybody what to do means they're handling whatever is happening above our heads. And then, another sound creeps in. It's like a growl and hiss mixed together. It makes the hair stand up on the backs of my arms.

"What is that noise?" I ask.

We all look at the ceiling and it is Mr. Alex who answers my question.

"Vampires."

"They're inside?"

"It's—it's not possible," Mr. Alex says.

The noise grates inside my brain. I can't stand it.

"Where's Aaron?" I ask.

Suddenly, there's a loud scream, and then footsteps on the stairs. Mr. Alex turns to face the door. It opens and I halfway expect to see my mom or dad, maybe Miss Celia or 'Lita, but this is someone I don't recognize. She's short with long black hair and her eyes—her eyes are black as coals and swimming with red.

"Are we playing hide-and-seek?" she asks in a monstrous voice that has some of those terrible sounds I'd heard upstairs mixed into it. "I love games."

Mr. Alex shoves us behind him and me, Ced, and Jules push ourselves to the back of the pantry.

"You are not invited," Mr. Alex says firmly. "Any invitation to you is rescinded."

The vampire laughs, showing her elongated teeth. "You know the rules. You didn't extend the invite. You don't have the power to take it back."

Mr. Alex stands still, his feet planted. "Let the children go. They don't have anything to do with this."

The vampire shakes her head and takes a step forward. Her foot presses into a pile of smashed garlic and she rears back, her jaw unhinging, her face unnaturally long, but she doesn't move from the doorway.

Mr. Alex makes a sudden move, like he's going to swing on her, but she catches his hand and yanks him toward her. She pulls his arm down with one hand, then places her other hand on top of his head wrenching it down so that the smooth skin of his neck is exposed.

"Little children," the vampire coos. "Watch this."

She opens her mouth and sinks her fangs into Mr. Alex's neck.

Cedrick screams and just as he does the vampire is suddenly snatched backward out of the pantry and into the basement. Aaron stands over her, shifting from a smoky black haze to his vampire form. Mr. Alex crumples to the ground. Cedrick rushes to him and cradles his head. Jules and I spill out into the basement.

Aaron struggles with the vampire as she claws her way toward us. Aaron grabs her legs but she turns her entire body into a swarm of screeching bats that surround Aaron. They fly into his face, tearing at his skin with their tiny claws. He furiously swats them away.

Jules takes a step forward. "Vampires hate the dawning day! For sunlight is the way they're slayed! Vanquish them and all undead! Nevermore shall we dread!"

I know the rhyme. It's not the little ones we learned in preschool. It's something more intense. Less like a nursery rhyme and more like a chant or a spell. It's something we didn't learn until we were older.

Both Aaron and the other vampire stop and turn toward Jules. The woman begins to repeat the rhyme but she's saying it so fast I can barely make it out. Aaron looks bewildered, like he can't understand what he's hearing.

I don't want Aaron hurt or confused but the other vampire shakes herself out of her stupor and I scream at her. "Bulbs of garlic! Holly branches! Silver shavings! Sunlight dances!"

"Don't invite them through the door!" Jules screams as their voice cracks. "Keep me safe forevermore!"

"Grab Aaron!" I shout as the woman lapses into confusion again. I pull the little black orb out of my pocket and hold my finger to the button.

Jules grabs Aaron and pushes him into the pantry. They glance at me.

"Close the door!" I yell.

"Boog!" Jules shouts. "Get in here!"

"Close the door!" I scream.

Jules hesitates, then slams the door shut. I push the button and close my eyes at the same time. There's a loud *pop,* a rush of warmth like when you walk in front of an open oven. I drop the orb. The light is brilliant even through my closed lids. I stagger back and fall hard onto the floor, pressing my hands to my face. There's a noise like a scream and a growl mixed together, and as the light dims, there's a smell of something burning.

I open my eyes and as the room comes into focus, there's a pounding of footsteps on the stairs. I scramble to my feet, putting up my fists, ready to punch a vampire straight in its ugly face, but it's my mom and Mr. Ethan.

Their gaze moves from me to the spot where the vampire is—or was. I'm confused by what I'm looking at. It's the size and shape of the vampire who'd attacked us but she isn't moving. Her entire frame is burnt to a crisp. She's now just a statue made of ash and Mr. Ethan immediately goes over and knocks it down. The ashes break apart and scatter on the floor. My mom rushes to me and wraps me up.

"Baby!" she cries. "Boog, baby, you okay?" She slides her

hands over my neck, checking for puncture wounds and it reminds me of the terrible thing hidden behind the pantry door.

I shake my head because I can't get the words out.

"Where's Cedrick?" Mr. Ethan asks, his gaze darting around the basement. "Jules? Alex?"

I just point at the pantry.

Mr. Ethan is there in a blink, throwing open the door. My mom gasps as Mr. Ethan drops to his knees.

Aaron is in the back of the pantry. Jules is covering him with their body but some of the skin on his arms and face is singed. Cedrick, his face streaked with tears, is cradling Mr. Alex's head in his lap and Mr. Alex presses his hand against his own neck, eyes closed, talking softly to Cedrick.

"It's okay," Mr. Alex says. "It's all going to be okay, Ceddy."

"He's hurt," my mom says, like she doesn't want to say what we can all see but I can't stay quiet anymore.

"He got bit," I say.

A deathly silence swallows the room.

Mr. Ethan quickly glances at Aaron and I break my mom's grip to tell him Aaron didn't do it, Aaron would never, but Mr. Alex reaches up and grabs Mr. Ethan's wrist.

"He saved me," Mr. Alex says in a weak, raspy voice. "Him and Boog and Jules." He turns his face up to Ced. "And Ceddy, too."

"Tre! Lidia! Celia!" my mom yells.

They all descend on the scene and I feel like I'm watching

it from outside myself. My mom says something but to me it sounds muffled.

My dad and Mr. Ethan pick up Mr. Alex and as they struggle to balance him, Aaron wraps Mr. Alex up.

"I'll take him up," Aaron says. He disappears with Mr. Alex, and my dad and Mr. Ethan race upstairs to help out.

'Lita, sword in hand, its blade black with something wet and sticky, gathers up Jules and smothers them with kisses as Jules sobs. Miss Celia takes Cedrick in her arms and all but carries him up the stairs. My mom stays with me and we are the only two left in the basement.

"Boog," she says.

I look into her face. I'm suddenly teetering on the edge of being numb and feeling everything. I can smell the burning remains of the vampire and I can still feel the heat from the Vanta-black orb.

"Mom?" I ask. "Is Mr. Alex gonna die?" A knot claws its way up my throat and I want to scream.

My mom grips my shoulders. "No. No, I won't let that happen." But after she says it she presses her lips together like she's not sure she's telling the truth. "Let's get upstairs so I can help him."

Miss Celia and 'Lita stand watch at the front and back doors as my dad patrols the yard outside. He keeps his set of shining razor-sharp stakes secreted under his coat. Jules and I pull a rug over a burnt patch of carpet in my living room. Apparently, another vampire had met a grisly end right on that spot. The mood in the house is low like we're all whispering, staying quiet, and moving slowly. My parents, with Aaron's help, had moved Mr. Alex into our spare bedroom upstairs. Mr. Ethan and Cedrick don't leave his side for one single second even though Mr. Ethan asks Cedrick repeatedly to go out of the room. Jules and I stand in the hallway outside the door and peer in as my mom and Miss Kim buzz around Mr. Alex.

"We can't stop the change in its tracks," my mom says. "But maybe we can slow it down until we figure something else out."

"The change?" Cedrick asks. "What—what do you mean?"

Mr. Ethan pulls Cedrick close to him. "Cedrick, your dad is AB negative."

A chill runs straight up my back. Jules's mouth opens into a little o. We all know what that means. Our vampire history lessons taught us that the only reason vampire numbers were low enough to vanquish them completely was because only people with an uncommon blood type could be turned—AB negative. Aaron had that blood type, too. As I look at Mr. Alex lying there, I realize that's probably why he was close to the Vanquishers but never a Vanquisher himself—it was way too risky to have someone with AB negative blood on the team. He could be turned into a vampire and then what? They'd have to vanquish him, too?

"I have the serum I give to Aaron," Miss Kim says. "I don't know if it will be helpful at all. It's for someone who's already a vampire."

"Maybe we could modify it somehow?" my mom asks. I can almost see the wheels turning inside her head as she tries to come up with a solution. "The process that causes someone to turn into a vampire is due to the rapid replication of the vampiric cells. They divide and replicate faster than any other virus or bacteria known to science. If we could slow it down, even just a little, it might buy us time?"

"Is it possible that if we hold off the change long enough it just won't happen?" Miss Kim asks.

"No," my mom says. "I don't think so."

"You're gonna help him, though, right?" Cedrick asks through choked sobs. "Please? Please, Mrs. Wilson. You gotta help him."

I walk into the room and put my arms around Cedrick and Mr. Ethan, who can barely do anything besides cling to each other. I want to go back and make it so that none of this ever happened but I can't.

"We're gonna fix this." I don't know if it's the right thing to say but I have to say something. "It's gonna be okay."

"I would already be on my way to the upper room if it weren't for Aaron," Mr. Alex says. His voice is low and raspy. He stares straight up at the ceiling and grips the bedsheet at his side like he's in pain but he keeps his voice steady. "Samantha, you gotta promise me you'll make sure he doesn't feel like any of this is his fault. Promise me." His pleading sounds so much like Cedrick's it breaks my heart so bad I want to cry.

My mom keeps her gaze fixed on her notes and on the screen of her laptop, which she has hauled into the room and set up on a small desk in the corner. "Stop talking to me like you aren't going to be able to tell him that yourself," she says. She's not trying to be mean but sometimes when she's upset, she's so blunt it comes across that way. She holds a lot of stuff in. "You're going to be fine because I won't allow it to be any other way."

Jules and I exchange glances and I know they're thinking the same thing I am—I don't know if my mom, with all her skills and abilities, has the power to make sure Mr. Alex will be fine.

My mom and Miss Kim talk about chemical compounds and looking at stuff under microscopes and I don't really understand any of that so I go back out into the hall, where noise draws my attention to the other end of the hallway. I see Aaron there, engulfed in shadows. The flecks of red in his eyes glow in the dark but his face is his own and it is a mask of sadness. Jules follows me as I walk over to Aaron and hold out my hand. He takes it and squeezes it tight. I notice that the skin that had been singed by the Vanta-black orb is almost completely healed.

"Mr. Rupert is downstairs," Aaron says quietly. "So I'm up here."

"This is such a bad time for him to be here with his old-man temper," Jules says, shaking their head.

I agree with Jules. I just hope he's not here to start any mess. Now is not the right time.

"Is Cedrick's dad gonna be okay?" Aaron asks. "If I had gotten down there sooner, I could have—"

"This isn't your fault," I say. Mr. Alex is right, and if he can't let Aaron know that, I will. "This doesn't have anything to do with you."

"I could feel them coming toward the house," Aaron says. "It was like my bones were humming. I felt it before. That night those other vamps attacked us at my house, but I didn't know what it meant. Now I know, and I should have done something sooner."

"Stop it," Jules says firmly. "That vampire would have killed Mr. Alex and probably the rest of us if you hadn't been there. You helped save Mr. Alex and now Boog's mom and your mom have time to try and help him. You're one of the good guys, Aaron. Don't think for one second that we don't know that."

Cedrick suddenly appears in the hall. He wipes at his eyes with the back of his hands and comes up to us.

"I could use a hug right now, y'all," Cedrick says.

We all gather around him, holding tight to each other and to him. Aaron tries to hang back but Cedrick reaches out, grabs the front of his shirt, and pulls him close. We don't say anything for a long time but we're all feeling the terrible ache of worry for Mr. Alex.

"How did they even get in?" Mr. Rupert's voice echoes from downstairs.

"They had Casey," 'Lita says.

I break away from the group and move to the landing, being careful not to tread on the creaky step. I'm about to try and ease past it when I'm suddenly surrounded by a cloud of cold dark air. Aaron has me around the waist and is holding me so that my feet dangle above the floor. As we hover silently in the air we listen carefully to the conversation happening below.

"How?" Mr. Rupert asks. He sounds annoyed as per usual.

"We were all meeting here," 'Lita says. "They—they had him and they said they would kill him if we didn't invite them in. Tre extended the invitation but as soon as they were inside he tried to rescind it. They knocked him unconscious."

There is a loud exhalation but I can't tell if it's Mr. Rupert or 'Lita.

"This is what happens when you try to do things differently!" Mr. Rupert shrieks. "You have a vampire in this house at this very minute! You invite them in!"

Mr. Rupert suddenly goes completely quiet. Aaron, still holding tight to me, floats us silently a little farther down the stairwell so we can peek into the living room. When we do,

'Lita is standing over Mr. Rupert as he cowers on the couch, but she is staring us dead in the face.

"Go back up!" I say in a whisper that I'm sure everybody in the immediate vicinity can hear.

Aaron floats us back up the stairs like we didn't just try to eavesdrop on what was meant to be a private conversation.

CHAPTER 10

The news picks up the story of what happened at my house and I brace myself for a return to the way things were before the Reaping. I wonder how we'll manage school and what the nightly lockup routine will look like if we all have to go back to vamp-proofing our lives. Could it be any more detailed than what we're already doing? And even the steps we've already taken didn't keep us safe, so what now? But that's not what happens at all.

As I sit in front of the TV in my living room with Jules and Cedrick at my side, the news anchors tell a story about vampire wannabes—people who want so badly to be vamps that they file their eyeteeth into points, wear black contacts, and pretend to drink blood. The news is saying that they are the ones who are responsible for what happened at my house and that the injuries to Mr. Alex aren't life-threatening. Nobody corrects them. My mom says it's because that is the story people want to believe. That the general public would do anything to keep living their vamp-free existence even if it means ignoring the truth. She also says that *we* are clearly the targets of this new hive. The truth is that the reemergence of these new vamps and the only two recorded attacks in the past twenty years have occurred right here on the street where all the remaining Vanquishers and their kids live. It is not a coincidence.

Cedrick flicks his hand toward the TV. "So my dad's injuries are life-threatening?" he asks.

I touch Cedrick's shoulder. We know they are. Mr. Alex is still in the guest bedroom with my mom and Miss Kim keeping a constant vigil over him. They've given him a modified version of the serum that Miss Kim developed for Aaron. It appears to be keeping him from becoming one of the undead, but his body is trying desperately to make the change. His normally brown skin is ashen and his eyes have a darkness to them that makes everyone uneasy. None of us know how much longer my mom and Miss Kim will be able to keep him from changing.

I glance toward the little hallway that connects the side of my house to the garage. Aaron is resting in the storage room under our garage floor. My dad says it's too dangerous for us to be apart and even though Aaron's house is right at the top of the block, that's way too far. I'm counting down the hours until he can come out and I pass the time by diving back into the book I'd borrowed from Cedrick's dads.

I cradle it in my lap as I read through the last few entries, which have gone from sounding like they should be entries on Wikipedia about vampires and their habits to more personal accounts of what happened right around the time of the Reaping. There were entries from each of the Vanquishers. The last one is from my mom.

Carmilla
May 12, 2002
It is over. I can't really believe it. I don't know that I ever will. It had all come to this and here we are at the end of everything—broken beyond repair. We're urged to move on. How is that possible? There is more to say, more to be written, but I can't think straight right now. We'll take the time to mourn. How we move on without Dayside and Nightside is beyond me. Maybe we take this chance and make a better life for ourselves, but I don't think it can ever really be over for me, or any of us.

It lines up with the way I'd seen my mom behave my whole life—protective to a fault, watchful. She couldn't let the past go but it turns out she didn't need to, because it came right back around. I run my fingers over the lettering. Her words were so sad. I close the book and strum my fingers across the back cover, which is coming apart at the seam in the upper left-hand corner.

"What do you think is gonna happen now?" Jules asks.

I lean in and Cedrick angles his ear toward us but keeps his eyes on the TV.

"I don't know," I say. "But these vamps are after us or our parents or Aaron or whatever and we still gotta figure out who those guys with the symbol on their jackets were."

Suddenly there's a knock at my front door. Miss Celia is there before I can get to my feet. She holds something in her clenched fist. It looks like a small plastic cylinder. She angles it toward the door as 'Lita and my dad descend on the entry-way. They all have their weapons at the ready.

"Who is it?" Miss Celia calls through the door.

"It's me!" a voice shouts back. "Casey!"

'Lita rushes to the door and flings it open. Casey is standing on the front step swaying gently from side to side. My dad swoops in and catches him right as he collapses. As they drag him inside, I can see that he's terribly injured. His right eye is swollen and bruised. There is a large gash on his arm and a wound to his chest that's leaking through his shirt.

"What the heck happened to you?" Jules asks.

'Lita shushes them and waves us off as they lower Casey into a chair. They call for my mom and she comes running.

Her eyes widen and she gasps. "I would have bet any amount of money you were dead." She ducks into her office and returns a moment later with a small case. She slips on a pair of plastic gloves, then opens the case, removing a translucent piece of mesh. She opens Casey's shirt and lays the mesh over the wound on his upper right chest. He winces as the mesh clings to his skin with a vacuum-like seal.

"Are we sure I'm not actually dead?" Casey asks, groaning in pain as he readjusts himself on the chair.

"Don't say that," 'Lita says. She disappears into the kitchen and returns a moment later with a bag of crushed ice. She presses it to Casey's eye and he sucks in a chestful of air, like it hurts.

"The vampires . . . they took you and I—" 'Lita gets choked up as she helps tend to Casey's wound. "I'm so sorry, Casey. This is my fault."

Casey pats 'Lita's hand. "I got away. I learned from the best." He gives 'Lita a tight smile. "I had to pull out some moves from my days in the Wrecking Crew."

"What moves?" Cedrick asks.

Casey turns to him. "I've always been good in a bind. Close quarters are where I'm at my best. I can fight. The Vanquishers taught me."

Cedrick looks at Casey like he's small and Casey's brows push up.

"What's eating you, kid?" Casey asks.

'Lita puts her hand on Casey's shoulder. "Cedrick's father was bitten. He's fighting the change but—" She stops herself from saying any more.

Cedrick looks away and my heart breaks for him all over again.

Casey shakes his head. "I'm so sorry, kid."

Cedrick goes to the couch and sits. Me and Jules join him.

"I'm not trying to tell anyone what to do," Casey says through gritted teeth as my mom lays another sheet of the mesh over a small cut on his face. "But maybe you should teach the kids a little more than history lessons."

Miss Celia shakes her head and my mom huffs.

"They weren't even supposed to be a part of this," my mom says.

"But they are," Casey says. "It's too late for all that. They need to know how to fight."

"No," 'Lita says. "That's not how it's done."

Casey rolls his eyes and Cedrick gasps.

"He rolled his eyes at 'Lita," Cedrick says. "She's about to slice him up. Watch."

Jules nudges Ced in the side. "She only uses the sword on vamps."

"I feel like she should make an exception for him," Cedrick says quietly.

"I was a part of this, too," Casey says as he pulls himself to the edge of the chair. "I was there, playing my role, and I was left unprepared for my first encounters with the undead."

"History, defense, then offense," my mom says. "That's how it goes."

"I almost died a few times while you were waiting to teach me to fight," Casey says. There's an edge in his voice.

'Lita's hand drifts toward her waist and I am convinced she's about to make a kebab out of Casey right there in the dining room.

"You were *never* in that kind of danger," Miss Celia says. "We protected you."

"And where were you when this kid's dad was getting attacked?" Casey asks.

An awkward silence fills the room.

"That's not fair," I say.

"Grown folks' business, Boog," my mom says.

I shut my mouth but I want to yell in Casey's face.

Miss Celia trains her gaze on Casey. "You're out of line."

Casey starts to protest when my mom holds up her hand.

"No," she says. "Casey, you're right."

I whip my head around to look at her.

"The kids had to fend for themselves," my mom says as tears well in her eyes. "They weren't as prepared as they should have been and that's on me."

"We were prepared," I say, mean mugging Casey. "We had the rhymes and the orb."

"You gave them my orb?" Casey asks.

My mom sidesteps his question. "I'll talk to Mr. Rupert. Maybe some offensive training wouldn't be such a bad idea."

"Sam," 'Lita begins, but my mom cuts her off gently.

"I know what you're going to say, Lidia," my mom says. "I don't like it either. It's not the way we do things, but look at everything else that has had to change. We can't allow the kids to be in a position like they were last night. They did what they could." She quickly smiles at me. "But they need to know more in order to keep themselves safe."

"We've been trying to keep them safe this whole time," Miss Celia says quietly. "The only people we didn't really involve in that plan were the kids themselves." She sighs and puts her arms around 'Lita's neck. They look like each other and Jules looks like them. 'Lita sighs and nods at Casey, who turns and winks at us.

"Man," Cedrick says under his breath. "I wanted 'Lita to stab him."

At school the following Monday, the attack on my street is all anyone is talking about. Leighton and Adrianna gossip as we file into homeroom and take our seats. Adrianna is telling Leighton how her mom bought the best vampire repellant in the city and stockpiled it in their basement.

"What if other people need some?" Leighton asks.

"Too bad, so sad," Adrianna says, grinning. "We'll be protected and that's all that matters."

Leighton looks a little shocked that her so-called best friend sounds like she's not even worried about her.

"Anyway, I don't even think it's real," Adrianna says. "I think Boog and her stupid friends faked the whole thing to get attention."

Cedrick starts to stand up but I pull him back down to his seat.

"Don't," I say to him. "Remember what my dad said. People are gonna talk. Let them. Everything stays between us for now."

Cedrick gives Adrianna a look so dirty that Adrianna actually stops and stares at Cedrick for a few seconds in disbelief. She's usually so good at smiling her rotten little smile in your face when you try to mean mug her. Not this time.

Our parents were going to let us all stay home but they'd come up with a new treatment plan for Mr. Alex and wanted us out of the house while they tried it.

"This day is gonna be so long," Cedrick says. "I can already tell."

"Mr. Rupert is supposed to start the new lessons today," Jules whispers. "Do we put on our—our uniforms?"

"Are they uniforms?" I ask. "They're more like cargo pants."

"Reinforced cargo pants," Jules corrects. "And yes. They're uniforms."

"Well, I need to find a better pair of pants to go with my vest," Cedrick says. "Because jeans are too tight. How am I supposed to roundhouse kick a vampire in skinnies?"

"I don't think Mr. Rupert is going to teach us how to do that," I say. "Does he even look like he can teach us to fight?"

"I think I should fight him first," Cedrick says. "You know, to see if he has the right skills."

"And what happens when he whoops your butt?" Jules asks. "What then?"

Cedrick shrugs. "At least we'll know he can fight."

He laughs. It makes me happy to see him happy, even if it's just for a second. As soon as his thoughts turn back to his dad he'll be upset again and I'd do anything to keep him from feeling like that. Mrs. Lambert walks into the room and sets her things down on her desk.

"Good morning, class," she says cheerfully. "How is everyone doing?"

A chorus of murmured responses fill the room.

"I know there's a lot going on in the news." She glances at me and smiles warmly. "It would do us all some good to put our minds on something else for the time being." She leans on her desk. "Let's get to work, shall we?"

Mrs. Lambert runs through our plan for the week and helps us get organized. She informs us that all after-school clubs have been postponed. She doesn't say it's because of what happened at my house, but we all know there can be no other reason. It's the first time I'm seeing our school take any real steps toward keeping us safe from vamps and if I'm being honest, it makes me a little uneasy. We're just supposed to live under the threat of vampires all the time now, like that's not one of the scariest things in the world.

"I have a question," Leighton says, raising her hand.

Mrs. Lambert nods in her general direction.

"The people on the news are saying that the attack wasn't real vampires."

"Okay?" Mrs. Lambert says quizzically. "I thought you said you had a question."

Leighton turns and looks at me even though she's talking to Mrs. Lambert. "I want to know what the punishment is for pretending to be a vamp just to get attention. Like, what kind of clueless person would do that?" She grins at me and then immediately starts chatting with Adrianna. They both make sure I see them laughing at me.

I want to stand up and scream at them, tell them that not only is Aaron a real vampire but Cedrick's dad got bit and I watched the Vanquishers destroy a small hive of the undead monsters. But I can't say any of that.

"Vampires are extinct," Mrs. Lambert says. "So it stands to reason that the attack was in fact committed by people just like you've described. People seeking attention. People desperate to belong to something." She pauses and glances in my direction and I feel like I want to disappear. "But I can see, Miss Leighton, that you're not talking about just any people. You're talking about Boog and her family and friends. That doesn't seem fair. I think you should keep your unsolicited opinion to yourself."

Mrs. Lambert is always on my side. And yeah, she's telling Leighton to hush up, but she's also kind of agreeing with her. I sit quietly during the rest of class. When the bell rings I'm out of my chair first and heading for the door.

"Boog," Mrs. Lambert says. "Could you hang around for a minute? You and Cedrick and Jules, too."

I don't want to hang around. I want to get out of class and go call my mom from the office, ask her to pick me up, but I hang back with Ced and Jules. My classmates file out with both Leighton and Adrianna mean mugging me one last time. Mrs. Lambert lets everyone leave, then gently closes the classroom door.

"Are we in trouble?" Jules asks.

Mrs. Lambert shakes her head. "Not at all. I just wanted to talk to y'all for a second. Check in on you. Make sure you're okay."

I'd been a little annoyed with her for agreeing with some of what Leighton had said, but all that melts away when she smiles at us and gives my arm a gentle pat.

"We're okay," I say.

She narrows her eyes at me. "You can tell me if you're not."

Cedrick looks down at the floor.

"We're a little shaken up," Jules says.

Mrs. Lambert's expression softens. "Understandable. I hope the authorities find the people responsible."

I press my lips together to keep myself from saying what I'm thinking. *They weren't people. They were vampires.*

"Listen," Mrs. Lambert says. "I'm having a little get-together at the park by my house and I was hoping y'all would swing by."

"When?" I ask.

"Right after school. My sister is already there setting stuff up." She swats a fly away from her coffee cup. "You kids need something to get your mind off all this other stuff. I hate seeing you so down. It breaks my heart."

"We're not really allowed out anywhere right now," I say. "After what happened—"

"Don't even worry about it," she says. "I'll call your parents and make sure it's okay. We'll be done well before nighttime. What do you think? Sound like a plan?"

Mrs. Lambert wouldn't be inviting us if she knew the truth about Ced's dad, about all of it. But a party in the park doesn't sound half bad.

Jules and Ced glance at me like I'm the one who has to make the decision.

"I guess if we make sure it's okay," I say.

Mrs. Lambert clasps her hands together and does a little dance. "Great! Y'all go on to class. I'll call right now."

We shuffle off to our classes and when I have a break, I check my phone. There's a message from my mom.

MOM: Mrs. Lambert says she's having a get-together at Waverly Park right after school. You can go. I'll meet you there. We won't stay long.

A little wave of relief washes over me. I don't want to be too far from her right now and I know Cedrick wants to get back and check on his dad. But there's also a part of me that really wants to go. I want to pretend that things are the way they used to be for just a little while. I miss being out on my bike with my friends and only worrying about homework and what we're having for dinner.

After school, we walk the four blocks to Waverly Park. It's a newer park with barely used equipment and big open greenspaces with softball fields and no shortage of annoying kids. It's warm but the clouds are pushing in. Even still, walking the short distance to the park feels like a breath of fresh air after everything that has happened. Just feeling the warm breeze on my face and being out under the open sky is the best thing ever.

I lead the way to the pavilion where almost anybody who's having a get-together in the park sets up shop. I don't see Mrs. Lambert or her sister yet.

"I didn't even know Mrs. Lambert had a sister," Cedrick says.

"I've heard her say something about her once or twice," says Jules. "Remember that one time she was talking about how she went down to visit some family in—where was it? Florida?"

I can't remember the exact conversation but that sounds

right. I plop down on a bench at one of the picnic tables and look around.

"What kind of party is this?" I ask. "No decorations or nothing?"

Suddenly, I see Mrs. Lambert approaching the pavilion from the direction of the street. She doesn't have anything with her, but she's got a big smile on her face.

"Hey, y'all!" she says cheerily. "I am so sorry. My sister hasn't even gotten started putting up the decorations and with these clouds rolling in I don't know if I'm going to get to have my little get-together or not."

"Is there a special reason for it?" I ask. "Is it your birthday or something?"

"No," says Mrs. Lambert. "I just wanted to do something fun, you know? I'm cooped up in the classroom all the time and if I'm not grading papers I'm making lesson plans. I've been feeling like I need to make a better effort to do the things I really want to do."

"My mom calls that work-life balance," I say.

Mrs. Lambert smiles. "Do y'all mind helping me and my sister carry over some supplies? She's back at my house. It's not far. I just walked over. You can help us put up the decorations before we get rained out."

I hadn't realized Mrs. Lambert lives so close to the school.

"My mom is meeting us up here, so we probably shouldn't go anywhere," I say.

"It'll take fifteen minutes, tops," Mrs. Lambert says. "Oh. And y'all can meet my lizards."

Cedrick perks up. "I was wondering when we were gonna get a chance. Ever since that day we saw you in the pet supply store."

"Right! Did you know they're out of business now?" She shakes her head. "They had the best live food choices on the whole west side of town."

I recall seeing the abandoned store front when I'd gone on my little outing with Aaron.

"Come on," Mrs. Lambert says. "We'll go and come back before your mom even knows we left. And you're with me. I'll keep you safe."

A part of me is wondering what Mrs. Lambert really thinks about what happened on my street. If she had any thought that actual vampires were involved, there's no way she would have told me that she could keep me safe. The Vanquishers themselves could barely do that.

Cedrick hops up from his seat at the picnic table and follows Mrs. Lambert as she makes her way out of the park. Me and Jules follow close behind sharing concerned glances. I don't think any of us want to cause our parents any more trouble than we need to right now, but I also agree with everything that Mrs. Lambert said. We do need some time to get our minds off the heavy stuff even if it's just for a little bit.

In less than five minutes we are mounting the stairs of a

small blue house on a narrow street a few blocks from the park. I don't know what I thought Mrs. Lambert's house would look like but this isn't it. It's a ramshackle little place crammed between two other houses, one of which is completely abandoned. The house on the other side is in even worse shape than Mrs. Lambert's.

"Dang," Cedrick says under his breath.

"Watch the steps when you walk up," Mrs. Lambert says. "The boards are all loose. I keep meaning to fix them, but I just don't have the time or the money if I'm being honest. One day I'm going to fall straight through. I just know it."

I'm not judging anybody. I know better than that, but I'm concerned with why, with all the work Mrs. Lambert does for us at school, she isn't getting paid enough to make sure that the place she lives in is safe. I think of telling her that my dad could probably help her out with fixing the front stoop but I stop myself. I don't know if that would make things better or worse.

We continue up the front steps, avoiding the loose boards, and Mrs. Lambert unlocks her front door. We all hesitate at the threshold. Mrs. Lambert looks back at us.

"You need an invite?" Mrs. Lambert asks.

We cross over the threshold and as we do a chill runs straight up my back. Mrs. Lambert's house is freezing inside.

"What kind of AC you got, Mrs. Lambert?" Cedrick asks. "My house never gets this cold."

"It's a new unit," she says. "Just had it installed."

The inside of her house doesn't match the outside. I expect things to be a work in progress inside, too, but it's much more put together than the outside. She has a matching sofa and love seat in the living room and a big black rug covers most of the hardwood floor. She has paintings and knickknacks that all look like they're straight out of Dracula's castle—heavy brass candlesticks with bits of spent candles stuck in the sockets. Everything is dark—black and various shades of red. The walls are dark and a large mirror in a heavy gold frame hangs in the short hallway. The kitchen is just to the left and it's connected to a dining room where a round table sits piled high with unopened mail. The furnishing and decorations are dark but so is the house itself. None of the lights are on except for the one over the stove in the small kitchen.

"Where's the decorations, Mrs. Lambert?" Jules asks. "And your sister?"

Mrs. Lambert marches down the hall and looks through a door near the rear of the house.

"She must've left already," she says, looking a little confused. "She said she was gonna hang around here and see if those clouds mean rain or not. We didn't see her walking, right?"

We all shake our heads. Just then, a smell wafts into my face. I wrinkle up my nose and I almost put my hands over my mouth to keep the smell from hitting the back of my throat, but

I don't wanna be rude. Cedrick doesn't even pretend not to smell it.

"Dang!" he says. His entire face twists into a mask of disgust. "Smells like roasted turds in here, Mrs. Lambert."

Jules covers their face with their hands. "Oh my god, Cedrick, please shut up!"

"It's okay," Mrs. Lambert says even though she looks a little embarrassed. "It's the lizard cage. It's funky. I can't get used to it."

I can't remember how long she's had them, but I would think if she hated the smell she'd have found a way to deal with it by now.

"Come look at them," she says. "They're so cute."

I pad down the hall and peer into the room at the end. It's empty except for a large rectangular table. There are heavy, dark draperies obscuring the single window. On top of the table is a glass terrarium and scattered around on the floor are plastic wrappings and empty boxes. There are no less than five or six CatchPros positioned around the room; their bottom chambers are filled with flies and the buzzing sound bounces off the walls.

Cedrick goes up to the cage and peers through the mesh lid. "It's not really that funky up close."

Jules crowds in. "Please stop telling Mrs. Lambert her house stinks," they whisper. "It's so rude."

"It's true," Cedrick whispers back.

I walk over and peer into the terrarium. There are two medium-sized lizards squirming around inside and Cedrick's right. It's not really that smelly up close. There are some rocks on the bottom of the glass enclosure and an empty water bowl. There's a sticker on the outside of the glass that says SALE 39.99. The lizards circle around each other.

"Do they have enough room in there?" I ask. "I feel like they're too big to be sharing a cage."

I glance up and Mrs. Lambert is gone from the doorway.

Jules picks up one of the empty boxes. "It's for the water bowl."

"It's new?" I ask.

"I guess?" Jules says. They toe at one of the other boxes. "The wrapping for the rocks is here, too."

"But we saw her getting food for them weeks ago," Cedrick says. "Remember that? She was getting a bag full of roaches to feed them."

"Something's not right," I say quietly as a strange feeling settles over me. I'm suddenly really uncomfortable being here. "Why is everything new then?"

"I had to replace everything," Mrs. Lambert says. She's retaken her place in the doorway. She comes in and stands behind us. "They really do need a bigger enclosure. This one's bigger than the last one I had but it's still not big enough."

Something stirs in the pit of my stomach. At first, I try to brush it off, but it comes back stronger. Something is wrong.

"Mrs. Lambert," I say. My pulse ticks up. "Where's your sister?"

Mrs. Lambert stares into the cage. "I don't know, Boog. I'm a little worried, actually."

I put my hand on Jules's back and lean toward the cage. I look them dead in the face as our eye levels align. I blink twice and press my lips together. Jules's eyes grow wide.

"I kinda wanna go home," Cedrick says.

When I turn to face him he's wearing a blank expression and has taken a step toward the door. Cedrick is good for saying exactly how he feels but something in my gut is screaming at me to play it as cool as possible. Like if I move too fast or say the wrong thing, something bad—*really* bad—will happen.

"I'm wondering how your friend Aaron is doing," Mrs. Lambert says, mirroring Cedrick's steps and cutting off a path to the door. The room suddenly seems darker than it already was when we first came in. "Everyone is saying he ran away and came back on his own but I don't think anybody in this room really believes that." She sighs. "Has he been able to tell you anything about what really happened to him?"

"Mrs. Lambert, we gotta go," I say firmly. "My mom knows we're with you and that we're supposed to be at the park. We gotta get back."

A big, juicy fly buzzes into the room and lands on top of the terrarium. Mrs. Lambert stares at it.

"I'm sure she won't mind you being here," Mrs. Lambert says. "You know, Aaron should come back to class. He should be at school with the three of you—with the Squad. It just doesn't feel right without him." She stares into the glass enclosure one more time. "It's like Ben and Jerry here. They need each other the same way all of you need each other."

Cedrick's brows arch up. He opens his mouth to say something but I catch his eye and gently shake my head. I slip my hand around Jules's wrist, gripping it tightly. My other hand slips into my pocket. I pull out my phone and press it to my ear.

"I was just about to call you," I say to no one. "My phone's been on vibrate. Sorry. No. We're at Mrs. Lambert's house. I'll drop you my location." I tap around on my phone's screen and then press it back to my ear. "We'll wait outside. Love you. Bye."

Mrs. Lambert smiles but she doesn't move. My body tenses as my pulse speeds up. Am I really gonna have to fight my way out of Mrs. Lambert's house? And why is she acting like this? This is Mrs. Lambert. The best sixth-grade teacher in the school. Someone who has been on our side from the jump. Finally, after what feels like forever, she moves away from the door. As soon as she's clear of it, I back out into the hallway.

"I hate to see you go," Mrs. Lamberts says. "Sure you don't want to hang out? My brother will be back soon with the decorations."

"Your brother?" Jules asks. "I thought you said it was your sister."

That terrible feeling in my gut is like a blaring alarm now. It's screaming at me to get out. To run. I take another step back and the terrible smell that we thought was coming from the lizard cage wafts into my face again. Just off the main hallway is another room and its door is standing ajar. Inside is a bed, a small table with a lamp, and flies. Hundreds and hundreds of flies. That is where the smell is coming from. They are buzzing around the room in swarms. There is not a CatchPro in sight but there are several clear plastic bags on the bedside table—all of them squirming with roaches.

I book it toward the front of the house. The front door is locked. I can hear Mrs. Lambert's footsteps in the hall behind me. I pull back the deadbolt and we fall out onto the front stoop. We run all the way back to the park without stopping. My mom is pulling up right as we arrive and we dive into her car and lock the doors.

"Mom!" I shout as I look out the back window, half expecting Mrs. Lambert to be chasing after us like some monster out of a nightmare.

"Where were you?" my mom asks. "I thought you said we were meeting at the park."

"The lizards," Cedrick says quietly. "She called them Ben and Jerry but last time she said their names were Bert and Ernie."

CHAPTER 11

When we're safely back at my house I tell my mom everything. I tell her how weird Mrs. Lambert's house was and about the lizards, the roaches, the flies, and the smell.

"The smell?" my mom says. She's standing in the living room, her hands pushed down on her hips, her eyes narrow. "What did it smell like?"

"Like hot garbage," Cedrick says. "I thought she was roasting boo boo in the oven, Mrs. Wilson."

My mom bites back a smile. Then tilts her head up and looks at the ceiling. "I need to make a phone call. Cedrick, baby, go spend some time with your dad."

Cedrick goes upstairs to be with his dad, who is still holed up in our guest room.

"Miss Kim's serum is working then?" I ask my mom.

"Two and a half days of it are keeping him semi-stable, but it's a constant infusion now." She sighs. "We can't keep this up indefinitely."

It scares me to think about what that means, and I get up and put my arms around my mom's waist.

She squeezes me tight. "You're staying home tomorrow. And I think Jules and Cedrick should, too. I'll talk to Miss Celia and Mr. Ethan."

"Why?" I ask. "Because of Mrs. Lambert?"

She nods. "That's who I'm going to call. See if she can meet me tomorrow after classes are out. I don't like a single thing about what y'all told me. I'll straighten it out."

"I wanna go, too," I say. "Mrs. Lambert is my favorite teacher. She's never been weird with us until now."

"That might be true," my mom says. "But I think we all agree that a house full of flies and bags of roaches and the thing with the lizards—it's beyond weird."

"What do you think it means?" I ask.

My mom has a faraway look in her eyes. "I have a thought but we'll need to wait till tomorrow to see if I'm right."

As nighttime descends, Aaron emerges from his slumber and after a quick snack—some warm O negative and a racoon out on the Green—he joins us as we go into the basement for a meeting with Mr. Rupert.

We all stop dead in our tracks when we get to the bottom of the stairs. Mr. Rupert is wearing a sweatsuit.

I'm just trying to figure out if the outfit is something he had in his closet or if it's something he just bought. Either way, it's a terrible mistake. Aaron and Jules are trying not to laugh and Cedrick is looking at Mr. Rupert like he can't comprehend what he's seeing.

"Now, Mr. Rupert," Cedrick says. "Why are you dressed like that?"

"Do not start with me, Mr. Chambers," Mr. Rupert says. "Your parents have informed me that they would like you to learn some defensive and offensive strategies to go along with your growing knowledge of vampire lore and Vanquisher history. Today is your first lesson."

"And *you* are gonna be the one to teach us?" Cedrick asks. "Are you qualified?"

"Young man," Mr. Rupert says sternly. "I am as qualified as any of the Vanquishers."

I doubt it. I saw my mom do a full barrel roll as she was slaying the vamps who attacked us when Aaron was first changed. One time I saw Mr. Rupert get up from his chair and grab his back like somebody had stabbed him. They are not the same.

We gather in the basement and the tables and chairs are all stacked up. Some of the plastic mats from the school gym are spread out on the floor. I don't know what Mr. Rupert has planned but if he tries to make me wrestle my friends on this mat that smells like pee and armpit sweat, I'll stake him myself.

"Vampires have the ability to appear and disappear," Mr. Rupert says as he paces on the mat in front of us. He shoots an angry glance at Aaron but I think he knows if he says anything out of pocket, I'll tell on him as fast as possible. Little circles of sweat are spreading out from under Mr. Rupert's armpits and we haven't even done anything yet. "Your ability to anticipate their movements will be valuable," he continues. "You can fight them, but you will have to use a combination of observational skills alongside any close combat fighting techniques you learn." He points to the whiteboard where he's drawn the worst depiction of a vampire I've ever seen. There are red dots over the left chest and neck. "Prolonged exposure to direct sunlight will destroy a vampire as will a stake of silver or holly wood directly to the heart. Let's start with that."

Mr. Rupert positions me and Aaron across from each other and then pairs off Jules and Cedrick. He arms us with stakes that are the approximate size and shape of the stakes my mom and dad use in their weapons but ours are made of rubber.

"Where'd you even get these?" Jules asks.

"I made them," Mr. Rupert snaps.

Cedrick is pressing his lips together so tight to keep himself from laughing that it almost looks like he doesn't have any lips at all.

"Stand with your back to each other," Mr. Rupert says.

"Then I'd like one of you to spin around as quickly as possible while the other aims and strikes at the heart."

"What?" Cedrick asks. "Like spin in a circle?"

"No," Mr. Rupert says, frustration coloring his every word. "Spin and face the other person."

"Right," Cedrick says even though he's shaking his head no.

We do as he asks, pretending to stake each other in the heart. Aaron doesn't spin around. He turns himself to smoke and then reappears somewhere in my vicinity without warning. I gently poke him with the stake and he grins.

"That's actually quite helpful," Mr. Rupert says.

I exchange glances with Aaron. Usually, Mr. Rupert is either way too mean to Aaron or busy acting like he doesn't exist.

"Can you run that drill with both Jules and Cedrick?" Mr. Rupert asks.

"Sure," says Aaron.

He goes through the same motions with them and after a while we're all pretty good at hitting our target on Aaron's left upper chest.

"What about you, Mr. Rupert?" I ask. "Are you gonna practice?"

"That's why you're wearing the sweatsuit, right?" Cedrick asks, grinning. "So you can try and drop-kick Aaron even though it will definitely never work?"

Mr. Rupert glances at Aaron, who gives him a little nod.

Me, Ced, and Jules move off the mat as Aaron and Mr. Rupert stand face-to-face. Mr. Rupert grips the rubber stake.

"Do not be easy with me," Mr. Rupert says.

Cedrick rubs his hands together and leans close to my ear. "Aaron is gonna break him in half. Watch."

Aaron and Mr. Rupert stand still as statues as they stare each other down. Aaron suddenly disappears and reappears behind Mr. Rupert but Mr. Rupert is already facing him. Aaron moves to the right and so does Mr. Rupert. Aaron turns his body to an inky black mist but as he resumes his human form a few feet away Mr. Rupert swoops in and catches Aaron by the back of his shirt. He holds the stake over Aaron's chest.

"Dang," Cedrick says.

Mr. Rupert is faster and more agile than he looks. But there's something about it that bothers me. He looks mad, like this isn't just some practice session to get us ready to fight off the undead. When he looks at Aaron there is anger.

Aaron slowly glides away from Mr. Rupert, whose jaw is set, eyes narrowed.

"What?" Mr. Rupert asks. "You think I don't have what it takes to know your every move?"

Aaron tilts his head to the side. "It's not that."

"What is it then?" Mr. Rupert asks.

"You look at me like you hate me," Aaron says. "I didn't even do anything to you."

"Not yet," Mr. Rupert says. "But you cannot help what you are." He walks up to Aaron until they are so close Mr. Rupert is partially obscured by Aaron's bottom half, which is still a cloud of black mist. "Vampires are monsters."

"You don't know what I am," Aaron says. "I'd never hurt anybody."

Mr. Rupert sighs but his gaze never leaves Aaron. "I hope that's true. I hope you keep your word, but the word of a vampire means very little to me."

"Why?" Aaron asks.

"Because a vampire took my son from me," Mr. Rupert says.

It's like the air has been sucked out of the room. Nobody says a single word.

Mr. Rupert's jaw is set so hard his temple muscles bulge. He flares his nostrils, breathes deep. And then suddenly he lets his shoulders roll forward and he sighs again. "I told you I was at the Reaping, and that's true. My son was with me. His name—" Mr. Rupert's chin wobbles. "His name was Will. I hid him in a bookshop in the Pearl district during the last stand. I went to help your parents and when I came back I found him reciting a vampire rhyme as loud as he could. A vampire had entered the store and found Will and he kept him at bay. I stepped in, the trance it was in broke, there was a struggle, I couldn't save Will."

Tears well in my eyes. I can't think of a single thing to say. It explains at least some of why Mr. Rupert is the way he is. His own son was the boy he'd spoken about who held the vampire off with his use of the rhymes.

"I—I'm so sorry, Mr. Rupert," Aaron says. "I think I understand why you hate me."

"I don't hate you," Mr. Rupert says more gently than I've ever heard him speak before. "It's not your fault. I know that. But that doesn't make it any easier. I still have to look at you and when I do, I see little pieces of both who my son might have become and the thing that—that—" Mr. Rupert cuts himself off and walks away from Aaron, snatching up his coat and stomping upstairs.

"Oh man," I say. "You heard that?"

"No wonder he hates vampires so much," Aaron says. "A vampire killed his son."

We all sit quiet for a moment.

Jules is the first to speak. "I don't know about you, but now I feel bad for Mr. Rupert. No matter how rude and grumpy he is most of the time. Can you even imagine what that was like for him? And he saw it happen right in front of him."

Cedrick nods and rubs the tops of his arms. "It's so messed up."

For the first time since we met Mr. Rupert, I feel something other than annoyance or frustration when I think about him. I still think it's not okay for him to be so harsh with us, especially Aaron, but I get it now and I feel awful.

The next day me, Ced, and Jules stay home like my mom said we would and Mrs. Lambert calls to check on us. It sets something off in my mom, who has a hushed and hurried conversation with Miss Celia, who comes over in the late afternoon and announces that she and my mom are going to a parent-teacher conference with Mrs. Lambert.

We put on our shoes and wait in the back of my mom's car so they can't tell us no when we ask to go with them. When they pile into the car they don't even ask us what we're doing.

"See," says Ced. "We're the Wrecking Crew. We get to go on missions."

My mom stares at us in the rearview mirror. "This is a parent-teacher conference. You're supposed to be going with us. Your dad asked me to check on your homeroom grades while I'm up there."

Cedrick slouches down in the back seat. "Maybe this is a bad idea."

"Well, I'm not worried," Jules says. But if the expression on their face is any indication, they're actually very, very worried.

My mom backs out of the driveway. "Too late now. Y'all wanted to go on a mission. Well, here it is."

As we make the ten-minute drive to the school, I can't help but think of Mr. Rupert.

"Mom," I say.

She looks at me in the rearview mirror.

"How long have you known Mr. Rupert?"

She and Miss Celia exchange glances. "A long time. Why?"

"Did you know his son?" I ask.

My mom sighs. "Yes."

"Mr. Rupert told us about what happened to him."

There is a long pause. "I figured it would come up eventually, but it wasn't my place to say it."

"I think it's why he hates Aaron so much," I say. "It's why he's so against doing things differently, right?"

My mom nods.

"It was a really dark time for him," Miss Celia says. "I can't think of anything worse than that."

Neither can I.

We finish our conversation just as we're pulling up to the school. The last of the teachers are filing out and driving off but Mrs. Lambert's car is in the parking lot alongside a few others.

My mom leads us up to the front door. We ring the bell but I can see through the glass that there is no one in the front office. My mom presses the bell again. This time the door creaks open and Mrs. Lambert appears in the space.

"Come on in," she says cheerfully. She pushes the door open wider and smiles at me. "Missed you all today."

It's weird that she's talking to us like she didn't try to trap us in her musty old house with a bunch of flies and roaches. I'm hoping it's because she has a really good explanation. I don't say anything to her as she leads us down the hall and into our homeroom class. She sits at her desk as my mom goes into the room. We follow her in and Miss Celia follows behind, kicking out the wooden block that holds the classroom door open and it slowly shuts by itself. Mom and Miss Celia sit in two plastic chairs that have been positioned up front. Cedrick, Jules, and I take our regular seats.

"Thank you for meeting us," my mom says. "I know it's last minute so I really appreciate it."

"It's no problem," Mrs. Lambert says. "I hope this isn't about what happened at the park. That situation was completely my fault and I am so sorry for causing you any kind of distress."

"It's fine," my mom says, but there's a ring in her voice. "We're actually here to talk to you about something else altogether."

I glance at Cedrick and Jules but they look just as confused as I feel. I really thought we were here to talk about how Mrs. Lambert almost had us trapped in her smelly house and how weird she was acting while we were there.

"We were told that there were some questions being asked about Aaron," Miss Celia says. "What happened to him has been all over the news but we understand you have a different theory?"

I slide down in my chair and try to become invisible. My mom and Miss Celia are going to bring up everything we told them right here in front of us and I am so embarrassed.

"I'm not sure I get your meaning," Mrs. Lambert says. "I did ask about Aaron of course. I'm his teacher. I'm concerned about his safety and well-being."

"He's disenrolled," my mom says, her tone darkening. "So

you aren't technically his teacher anymore but I do understand the sentiment."

Miss Celia removes her purse from her shoulder and sets it on her lap. She unzips it and sticks her hand inside. My mom is sitting straight up in the chair. Her back isn't even touching the seat. That strange feeling stirs in my gut again. The feeling of something being very, very off.

"I care about all of my students even after they move on to other schools or other programs," says Mrs. Lambert. She leans back in her chair and tents her fingers under her chin. "I'm sorry, Mrs. Wilson, but I actually can't talk to you about Aaron at all. Confidentiality laws would make that improper. Malika is your child and therefore she should be your only concern."

In any other situation those would be fighting words. I wait for my mom to respond with the same disrespectful energy Mrs. Lambert is giving but something even worse happens— she just smiles, which I know means things are about to go left in the worst way.

Several flies buzz around the room and my mom swats at them as they come close to her. "Administration really should do something about these flies," my mom says. One flies very near to her face, then lands on the back of her hand, which rests on her knee. She smacks it and its crumpled body falls to the floor.

Mrs. Lambert sits up straight behind her desk. "I'm sorry,

Mrs. Wilson, but I think we may have to cut this meeting short. I'm a little behind on grading papers and I—I really need to get caught up."

Miss Celia scoots to the edge of her chair and from her purse produces a small clear container. Something brown and furry runs in frantic circles inside it. Miss Celia leans forward and sets it on Mrs. Lambert's desk.

"Mom?" Jules asks. "Is that a mouse?"

My mom is on her feet now and so am I. More flies buzz around Mrs. Lambert's desk as she sits still as a statue.

"I'm wondering how you can even stand to be in this room at this very moment," my mom says to Mrs. Lambert. "All of these flies. All these tender, tiny little lives just waiting for you to devour them."

A fly lands on Mrs. Lambert's desk. She raises her hand and smacks it hard. The flattened fly sticks to her palm as she presses her hand to her mouth.

Cedrick and Jules are on their feet and at my side in the blink of an eye. Miss Celia moves in front of us but I can still see Mrs. Lambert. She chews the fly like she's chewing a piece of gum, swallows it, then closes her eyes and sighs.

"Did she—did she just eat a fly?" I ask.

"I guess you've found me out, Mrs. Wilson," Mrs. Lambert says. "How?"

"Doesn't matter," says my mom. "Who do you serve?"

Serve? I struggle to make sense of what's happening.

Mrs. Lambert stands up and moves around her desk. My mom stands directly in front of her.

"Oh, I'm afraid I can't share that information with you . . . Carmilla." She turns to Miss Celia. "Or you either, Argentium."

I gasp so hard one of the flies almost gets sucked into my mouth. She knows my mom is Carmilla. She knows my mom is a Vanquisher.

"Mrs. Lambert?" I ask as the full weight of her betrayal starts to weigh on me. But there's something else. Something I'd seen in a movie, or maybe it was a book. It rushes to the front of my brain and it's suddenly clear. No. It was something Mr. Ethan told me. Dracula was the big bad in the story, but he didn't do his terrible deeds alone. He had help.

"She's a familiar," I whisper.

My mom's gaze darts to me and I swear I see a smile flit across her lips.

Miss Celia nods. "She serves a vampire. The leader of this new hive, probably."

"What were you promised?" my mom asks. "The vampire you serve, did they promise you that you could become like them? Is that really what you want?"

Mrs. Lambert snatches another fly out of the air and shoves it in her mouth. Her gaze darts to the mouse in the container on her desk and she eyes it greedily.

"None of that is your business," Mrs. Lambert snarls. "All

you need to know is that none of you are safe. You never will be. And you have only yourself to blame."

Mrs. Lambert reaches for the mouse and Miss Celia knocks it away from her. Mrs. Lambert looks at me and I feel like I'm seeing her for the first time.

"Boog," she says.

But she doesn't get a chance to say anything else because my mom grabs her by the front of her shirt, spins her around, and shoves her so hard she flies into the window. The glass shatters, falling to the floor in a shower of broken shards.

Mrs. Lambert climbs to her feet, panting, sweat trickling down her forehead. Miss Celia lunges toward her but instead of heading for the classroom door, Mrs. Lambert scrambles out the broken window, cutting her hands on the jagged pieces of glass still sticking out of the frame. As soon as her feet hit the ground she sprints off and disappears around the side of the building.

The drive home is like real-life *Super Mario Kart*. My mom navigates the streets so that she doesn't have to hit a stop sign or a red light and she may or may not have hit a curb and a trash can along the way. When we pull into the driveway she's got her door open before we come to a full stop. She positions our car close to the wall in the garage so that the secret doors in the floor can open when Aaron is ready to get up. Miss Celia ushers us out of the car and into the house, while my mom calls out for my dad. As soon as we're in the living room, Miss Celia disappears to find 'Lita.

Once everyone is gathered, including Mr. Rupert and a very tired and hopeless-looking Mr. Ethan, my mom stands in the center of the room and tells everyone what happened.

"Mrs. Lambert is a familiar," she says in a deadly serious tone.

"Excuse me?" Mr. Rupert asks. His jaw is hanging open. "She's a *what*?"

Cedrick looks at Mr. Rupert. "Do you not know what that is or—"

"Of course I know what it is!" Mr. Rupert snaps. "A familiar has been in our midst this entire time and we're just now finding out about it? How is that possible?"

"Pipe down, Daniel," my dad says.

Mr. Rupert throws his hands up in defeat.

"Everyone keeps saying 'familiar,' " Jules says quietly. "What does that mean, exactly?"

There's a pause, like they're considering not telling us about it.

"Malika picked up on it, too," my mom says. She gestures to me like I should be the one to tell it.

I turn to Ced and Jules. "A familiar is a person who is in service to a vampire. I put it together too late but I remembered what Mr. Ethan said when we were looking at that stuff in Ced's basement. Dracula had Renfield, a helper."

"Dracula is a made-up story," Cedrick says.

I wait for someone to reassure Ced that it's true, that Dracula is just an old scary story and that he doesn't need to worry but nobody does. Nobody says anything. In fact, everybody gets weirdly quiet.

My dad leans close to Mr. Rupert. "Have you covered Van Helsing yet in any of your lessons?"

Mr. Rupert shakes his head.

"Wait," I say, my mind twisting itself in a knot to understand what they're getting at. "Are you—are you saying it's not a made-up story?"

"Now is not the time," Mr. Rupert says.

My head goes blank. Jules and Cedrick are speechless, just sitting there with their mouths hanging open.

"Getting back to the issue at hand," 'Lita says. "Boog is right. Familiars serve powerful vampires, usually with sinister motives. Vampires, even at their strongest, cannot be awake every single hour of the day. They use the familiars as their eyes and ears when they cannot be present."

"Why was she eating flies?" I ask. I try to push all thoughts of *Dracula* to the back of my mind but we're gonna have to have a serious conversation later. I put my thoughts on Mrs. Lambert. I think of all the times she had complained about the flies, how she promised she was going to have someone find out why so many of them were gathered in our classroom. It occurs to me that she probably lured them there herself so she could have an afternoon snack.

Mr. Ethan rubs his temple. "She has the hunger?"

My mom nods and turns to me. "Sometimes a familiar is just a person who has chosen to belong to a vampire, to do its bidding by choice. But sometimes the connection between a vampire and its servant is more . . . complicated. I've seen enough to recognize that Mrs. Lambert has entered into one of these more complex relationships with a vampire." My mom takes a deep breath. "She has what we call the hunger. It means that she hasn't been bitten, but she has been given some quantity of vampire blood to drink. The blood came from the vampire she serves."

The thought of it makes me want to puke. "Why would somebody do that?"

"For humans," my mom says, "drinking the blood of a vampire can imbue that human with preternatural powers for a short period of time. On top of that, it establishes an almost unbreakable bond between the vampire and the human. The human cannot be free from the vampire no matter how hard they try unless the vampire who gave them the blood is vanquished."

"That's what Mrs. Lambert did?" Cedrick asks.

"Yes. And the flies . . . well." My mom shudders. "She now craves lives. Blood. Not in the same way a vampire does because she is not turned, but it's very similar."

"Gross," whispers Jules.

"And she knew who I was—who I am," my mom says.

Everyone's head snaps up and their attention is now focused on her. "She called me Carmilla. She called Celia Argentium. It is no coincidence that she teaches our kids. She's known all along." She looks around. "Where's Kim?"

Mr. Ethan points upstairs. "She hasn't left Alex's side. She's a saint."

My mom smiles but it's quick. "I'll talk to her but I think this gives us some idea where to begin if we're still trying to find the vampire who bit Aaron. Mrs. Lambert was there that night at the skate rink and she's been a familiar the whole time. I'd bet money she knows exactly who bit Aaron."

"All the time we were missing him and worried about him," I say, trying to put my thoughts together. "And she knew this whole time?"

"I can't be certain," my mom says. "But I really think she has been involved the entire time."

I can't believe it. I'm so mad at Mrs. Lambert I could scream.

"Where do you think she went?" Cedrick asks.

"Probably right back to the vampire she's serving," 'Lita says angrily.

"Which means she's told them, whoever it is, that we know about her," my dad says. "And that only puts us more at risk."

Miss Celia nods. "We're going to have to make some choices about what happens next. We're going to have to let the public know soon. This is too big of a threat."

"But they're still only after us," I say. "Mrs. Lambert is our teacher. Aaron is our friend. And these disappearances . . . they're not finding bodies. These vamps are building an army to use against us. Why?"

'Lita shakes her head, then sighs. "I think Boog is right but I cannot for the life of me understand why this should be happening now. After all this time."

Suddenly the doorbell rings and we all jump out of our seats. My dad moves to the door and after a moment lets Casey inside. As he closes the door, I catch a glimpse of the hazy orange sky. It's getting dark. I recheck the FangTime app and then listen for the familiar sound of Aaron coming through the hall from the garage. Sure enough, just as the sun is setting, he appears in the back hall and I pat the seat on the couch next to me. Mr. Rupert gets up and disappears downstairs.

"Your mom is upstairs," Mr. Ethan says to Aaron.

"Everybody's here," Aaron says. "What's going on?"

"Something came up," my mom says. Her tone is clipped and she has her arms crossed. "Boog, can y'all go upstairs, please? I need to talk to the grown folks for a minute."

I'm ready to have some time to talk to Ced, Jules, and Aaron alone, so we head up to my room. Aaron stops by the guest room to give his mom a hug and check on Mr. Alex, who looks like he's sleeping. He rejoins us in my room and I close the door.

"So Mrs. Lambert is working for a vampire?" Aaron asks.

"How'd you know?" Jules asks as they plop down on the floor.

"I could hear y'all talking," he says.

"From the garage?" I ask.

Aaron smiles. "If I concentrate really hard, I can hear a lot farther than that. Like down the block sometimes. That's how I knew those vamps were close by. I could hear them."

"Can you hear what they're saying downstairs?" I ask.

He grins and then tilts his head back to look at the ceiling. "Yeah. It's Casey talking. He's upset." His brow furrows. "He's pissed. Something happen to him?"

"Other than the fact that he got held hostage by some vampires and it looks like they used him as a pinata?" Cedrick asks.

Aaron listens intently. "He's saying he knows about DOVA. What's DOVA?"

"No clue," I say as I move closer to the door.

"He's asking if they knew all along," Aaron says. "If DOVA is responsible for exposing 'Lita's real identity."

Jules stands up. I grasp the door handle and turn it slowly. As I pull it open in one quick motion, it barely makes a sound. The air around me is suddenly cold and Aaron is helping me silently glide out into the hallway.

"Cool!" Cedrick says in a scream-whisper.

Jules gestures for him to be quiet and he claps his hand over his mouth. At the landing I listen intently.

"You have no idea what was happening," 'Lita says.

"I do now," says Casey. "Vampires have never stopped being a threat and you—you just let it happen?"

There's a *whooshing* sound like somebody has drawn a sword.

"Casey, you need to calm down and lower your voice," my dad says.

"You don't get to tell me what to do, Tre," Casey huffs.

"We have been vanquishing in secret for years," my mom says. "We never fully retired. How could you think that we would allow an edict from DOVA to make us abandon our oaths. We know what our responsibilities are."

I turn and stare Aaron in the face. They knew vampires weren't extinct?

"There was a point in time, right before the Reaping, that we had them nearly eradicated," Miss Celia says. "But other circumstances came into play. Things you don't know anything about."

"DOVA wanted the vampires gone," 'Lita says. "Every last one of them, except the ones they were experimenting on. We couldn't go along with what they wanted. They forced our hand. After the Reaping *they* decided we would retire and the message to the public would be that we had accomplished our mission—that the vampires were gone forever."

"And you knew they weren't," Casey says.

"Anywhere there was a rumor of a hive, we were there," my dad says. "We never stopped being vigilant. Most places we showed up, there was nothing. We vanquished the stragglers we came across."

There's a shuffle of feet, then Mr. Rupert's voice echoes up the stairs. "How do you know about any of this?"

"None of your business," Casey snaps.

I shake out of Aaron's grip and descend the stairs. I know I'll be in trouble for eavesdropping, but I don't care.

"Are DOVA the guys with the symbols on their coats?" I ask as I saunter down the steps and insert myself directly into grown folks' business.

"How do you—" Casey starts, but my mom shushes him.

"Boog, this is not the time," she says.

"I thought we were gonna stop keeping secrets from each other," I say as a little rush of anger pulses through me. "I've been reading the entries in those books. I know how scary dealing with vampires is and I get it. We can't be in on everything, but I saw those guys with my own eyes."

My mom sighs and shrugs. "They're from an organization called DOVA—Department of Vampire Affairs. They're a division of the government formed specifically to monitor vampire activity."

"You're just telling them outright?" Casey asks. "They're kids. They haven't even really been training and you're just telling this stuff? You never told me those things. You never gave me what I needed to keep myself safe!"

"This is different," my mom says. "These are our kids."

"Oh!" Casey says in mock surprise. "Right. Okay so that makes them special."

"Yes," my mom snaps. "It does!"

Miss Celia huffs. "Grow up, Casey. We wanted to keep you safe and you're mad because, what? You never got to be a Vanquisher?"

"That was my right!" Casey shouts. "That's what I was owed!"

Mr. Ethan stands and marches up to Casey. "Nobody is owed a title. Nobody. That's not how it worked and you know that."

"There's something else," I say, cutting them off. Telling them what I saw at the warehouse means exposing that I've gone against the rules . . . again. But it also means exposing Casey, because something is not adding up with him.

"What is it?" my dad asks.

I look down at the floor. "I—I followed Casey when he left Aaron's house because he's been acting weird."

"Excuse me?" my mom says. "Malika Shanice Wilson, tell me you did not leave the house unprotected—"

"It was my fault," Aaron says as he appears next to me in a burst of cold air. "I took her."

"See, so technically I wasn't unprotected," I say. I don't look at my mom. "Aaron kept us shielded when we were flying—"

"Flying?" my dad asks, his eyes wide.

"No not—not flying," I stammer. "Maybe flying a little. Just a little bit. But I was safe, I swear."

"That is not the point!" my mom snaps. "How could you

do something so dangerous? You know what's going on right now."

My dad puts his hand on my mom's shoulder and she shrugs him off. 'Lita stands up and approaches me. I keep my gaze trained on the floor.

"What were you saying about Casey?" she asks.

I glance at Casey, who has edged a little closer to the door. "He went to that big warehouse on the other side of town," I say. "The one with the symbol on it. He walked right up to the gate and spoke to the same two people who were at Mom's office. They acted like they knew him."

Everyone seems to forget that me and Aaron were flying through the sky like superheroes as soon as I reveal this little bit of information. They all turn to Casey, even Mr. Rupert.

"Casey," my mom says. "Tell me you're not working with DOVA."

'Lita physically cringes, like she's trying to get away from the words my mom just spoke.

"We trusted you," my dad says just above a whisper. "Treated you like family."

"Wait," Miss Celia says. "Casey. Does DOVA know about this new hive?"

Casey looks at her and smiles. "Of course they do." He looks me dead in the face, then touches his ear. It's only then I notice a thin, almost translucent cord going from his ear to the collar of his jacket. "Now," he says.

There is a thunderous rumble from somewhere outside. It shakes the house so violently I have to grab on to the couch to steady myself.

"All hands!" my dad shouts.

"Aaron!" my mom shouts as she shoulders her crossbow. "How many?"

Aaron tilts his head up, closes his eyes. When he levels his gaze at my mom, his face is pinched, his jaw unhinges, and his eyes swim with flecks of red as the whites turn black.

"Mrs. Wilson," he says in a voice that is not his own. "There—there are too many to count."

My mom rushes to the closet and swings it open. She tosses something to my dad and then something else to Miss Celia. Then, she pulls out a billowing red cape and pulls the matching cowl down over her face so that only her eyes are showing.

"Aaron, get Boog upstairs." She looks at me. "Get your stuff on! Be ready to move!"

Aaron grabs me and suddenly I'm in the upstairs guest room. Mr. Alex is still lying in the bed and Miss Kim is frantically bottling some of the serum she'd been producing for him.

"Something is happening," she says. "What is it?"

"I—I don't know," I say.

Jules and Cedrick come rushing into the room.

Mr. Alex rolls onto his side, groaning. He looks awful, like he hasn't slept in days. An IV sticks out of his arm and the green serum flows into him. The bag holding it is almost empty.

"Alex! Stay down!" Miss Kim shouts. "I need to keep your infusion going!"

"Lock the door," he says.

"Wait!" I say. I turn to Aaron. "We need our stuff, the Wrecking Crew gear!"

"Where is it?" Aaron asks.

"In a duffel bag in my closet."

He disappears in a cloud of smoke and a moment later he's tossing me the bag.

Me, Jules, and Cedrick shrug into our uniforms. Cedrick's tactical vest fits over his sweatsuit. Me and Jules change, slipping into our reinforced clothing and boots. It all feels stiff and bulky but Mom said it would help protect us. We have a ton of vampire lore and one fighting lesson under our belts. It doesn't feel like enough but here we are—the Wrecking Crew, suited up and ready to do what we can. The book Ced's dads let me borrow is hanging out of the bag. I roughly shove it back inside and sling the bag across my back.

From outside, that terrible sound echoes again, the same one we'd heard when the vampires attacked us only a few days ago—unnatural hissing and growling. This time, it's louder.

"There are so many of them," Aaron says, and even as his face transforms into something terrible, there is fear written all over it.

"Do you have anything defensive?" Mr. Alex asks from the bed. He's sitting up now. His face is oddly angular and the hollows under his eyes are deep and purple.

Cedrick pulls a few bulbs of garlic from his pockets and the silver chain 'Lita had gifted him.

"It's better than nothing," Mr. Alex says in a way that makes me feel like he doesn't believe it at all. "Crush the garlic and dress the doorframe with it," he says. He's hunched over now, holding his stomach like he might throw up.

I take the garlic from Cedrick and smash it under the sole of my boot. We scrape up the squished contents with our fingers and smear it over the entire doorjamb.

"The windows," Mr. Alex says. "Get them, too."

Cedrick handles one window while Jules takes care of the other. Miss Kim stands at Mr. Alex's side.

"I need more time to make another batch of the serum," she says. "If the infusion stops—"

"The only thing that matters to me are the kids," Mr. Alex says. "Do you understand me? Do what needs to be done to keep them safe. Promise me?"

Miss Kim nods. Cedrick runs to his dad and puts his arms around him. Mr. Alex rears back. Cedrick's hands are smeared with garlic and the places where it touched Mr. Alex begin to billow thick black smoke.

"Dad!" Cedrick shouts.

Mr. Alex shakes his head. "I'm fine. I'm fine." He raises his head and looks at Aaron.

I watch them watching each other. My heart sinks into the pit of my stomach. Mr. Alex looks the way Aaron did the first time I saw him after he'd been bitten—scared, uncertain . . . changed.

There's a thud on the roof right over our heads and little pieces of the ceiling fall down around us and land on the floor. There's a rush of footsteps on the stairs. The door swings open and standing there are the Vanquishers.

CHAPTER 12

The Mask of Red Death, her red skull mask glinting in the dim light from the hallway, her silver sword drawn. Carmilla, her crossbow at the ready, her bloodred cape and cowl draped around her. Threshold, his red mask and silver stakes glinting. Sailor's Knot, his mask white as bone except for the red eyes, has his length of glimmering silver-infused rope hanging from his belt loop. Argentium, her gray-and-white cape and cowl, her hands covered in a shimmering sliver powder, a Vanta-black orb hanging from her waist.

Cedrick, Jules, me, and Aaron stand shoulder to shoulder. I'm scared to death but there is a sense of purpose swelling in me that might just hold off my fears long enough to let us get out of here alive.

"The Wrecking Crew," my dad says as he looks us over.

"Look at y'all." There's sadness and worry in his tone as he and the others slip into the room.

"We can't hold them," 'Lita says. "But we have to get moving. Draw them away from the rest of the families on the street. We cannot allow them to hurt anyone else."

My mom moves to my side and I watch her gaze move over my outfit. "Here." She hands me a small vial of glinting silver dust. "Press the button to open the lid. Aim for the eyes, but any exposed skin will work. Got it?"

I nod. She hands Cedrick a small wooden stake and then hands Jules a silver one.

"I know I said I wanted to throw a stake in a vampire's neck but now I don't know," Cedrick says. Mr. Ethan hugs Cedrick, then moves to Mr. Alex's side.

"What's happening out there?" I ask, afraid to know the real answer.

Miss Celia puts her arm around Jules. "There is a horde of vampires attempting to breach our defenses. There are at least ten of them, probably more. Our defenses will not hold up much longer."

"What do we do?" Jules asks as tears cloud their eyes.

"We will do what we've always done," my dad says in an unwavering voice. "We will vanquish them."

Everyone begins to talk about how we're going to get out of here but I pull my mom to the side and speak to her as quietly as I can.

"I'm scared," I say as I look into her eyes.

She takes my face in her gloved hands. "Me too, baby. But we're going to get out of here, together."

"And go where?" I ask.

"There is a place. We can be safe there. Trust me." She kisses me on the top of my head and then turns to the group. "All right, Daniel is making his way to Tre's SUV. He will wait there for us. We'll move downstairs in groups. I'll take Boog. Ethan, you'll take Alex. Tre, you bring Cedrick. 'Lita and Celia will go with Jules. Aaron, baby, I need you to get your mom to the SUV. No stopping, no compromising. You see a vamp, you end it." She glances at Aaron. "I'm sorry, baby, not all of them are like you. The ones that are here right now are here to hurt us . . . bad."

"I know, Mrs. Wilson." His eyes turn to solid black orbs and his body becomes a cloud of black smoke. "I'll help however I can."

My mom nods, then looks to Miss Kim. "How long does Alex have before he needs another infusion?" Miss Kim doesn't answer. She just shakes her head like she's unsure. My mom blinks twice, glances at Mr. Alex, then sighs. "Okay," my mom says in a voice that is so much like a growl it scares me. "Let's move."

As soon as the door to the guest room is open, a wild-eyed vamp with long blond hair and skin so pale it's almost see-through appears on the other side.

"The Vanquishers? Hiding?" she says in a mocking tone.

My dad hurls a stake and it pierces her in the left side of her chest. She gasps, then disintegrates into a cloud of dust. She didn't even stand a chance. My dad turns toward me. I can't see his face but I feel like he's worried about what I might think. I give him a tight smile and he nods.

Aaron disappears with his mom and doesn't immediately reappear. I hope with everything in me that it only means he wants to stay with her at the SUV to protect her and not that something bad is happening down there.

'Lita steps into the hallway with Miss Celia and Jules at her heel. They move quickly down the stairs. I hear 'Lita shout, then the *whoosh* of her sword. "Move!" she yells.

My mom pushes my dad and Cedrick to the door and they follow 'Lita down. My mom tries to make Mr. Ethan and Mr. Alex go next but Mr. Alex refuses.

"It's gonna take me a minute to get down there," he says. "We'll catch up."

My mom nods and I think I see her look at Mr. Ethan in a weird way but she's pulling me along before I can question it.

The hall is dark. The lights are out now and shadows pull themselves across the floor. My mom reaches into the folds of her cape and produces something that looks like a flashlight. There's a soft *click* and the light that shoots out of it is like a beam of pure sunlight. She drags the light over one of the shadows and it begins to smolder. Hot gray smoke fills the hallway and I wave my hands in front of my face to try and clear it out. A long shadow darts up and smacks the light out of my mom's hand. It hits the floor and goes skittering into the dark. My mom pushes me behind her and from the smoldering shadow a figure emerges.

A vampire.

Goose bumps rise on my skin and my insides feel hollow. My teeth start to chatter as my mom crouches into a fighting stance in front of me.

The vampire's skin is scorched and looks like burnt paper on the entire right side of his face. His jaw hangs open and his fangs are bared. I feel like I can barely breathe but my mom's breaths are slow and steady.

"Vanquisher," the vampire snarls.

"Monster," my mom replies.

There's a strangled yelp from downstairs. I think it's my dad. I take a step toward the stairs but the vampire mirrors my movement.

"Run to him, Malika," the vampire says. "Save him."

My name from its terrible, gaping mouth is the worst thing I've ever heard.

"Speak her name one more time," my mom says. "See what happens."

The vampire peers at me in the dark and I swear his eyes turn red. The corners of his mouth pull up into a twisted grin. "Boog," he says, elongating the vowels and drawing out the word so that it sounds like a ghost wailing in the dark.

My mom shifts her weight and presses the crossbow into her shoulder. The vampire flinches. My mom lets the stake fly and it strikes the vampire in the arm. He grins again and turns himself to smoke before reappearing directly in front of my mom. He grabs the top of her head with his slender hand and wrenches it to the side, exposing her neck. She raises the crossbow in one quick motion, knocking the vampire back. He staggers, then lunges forward again, running full force into my mom. He hits her in the torso and she slams into me. We all tumble to the floor.

I roll over onto my back and scramble to my feet as my mom grapples with the monster on the hallway floor. She slams him against the floor and then he disappears and reappears behind her. He tries to slip his hands around her neck but she rolls out of the way and is up on her knees with the crossbow pointed at the vamp's chest. She pulls the trigger but the silver stake doesn't come out. My fingers curl around the vial of silver dust as my heart somersaults in my chest. I flip the lid open, pour the contents into my hand, and chuck it in the vampire's face.

His scream is like the howling of the wind during a tornado. The sound wraps around me and I quickly cup my hands over my ears. My mom yanks the silver stake out of her crossbow and embeds it in the vampire's heart. The vamp crumples to the floor, then disintegrates.

"Come on!" my mom says.

She grabs my arm and pulls me down the stairs. I miss the first few steps but my mom doesn't let me fall. Another vampire is writhing around in the living room, silver stakes pinning him to the floor. We move past him, toward the side door that leads through to the little hallway that connects the garage to the house.

My heart is galloping in my chest as we push through the dining room, where the chairs are all flipped over and the table is split clean in half. The front door is wide open and I get a glimpse of something moving in the glow of the streetlights right outside the gate in front of our house—people. No.

Vampires. Six, seven, eight of them.

Their wild eyes glint in the streetlight. Their mouths hang open, fangs bared. My mom sees them, too, and slows her step for a half second. Her eyes widen. Then she picks up the pace again. We race to the hallway and rush toward the garage door, which is off its hinges.

My mom kicks it aside and we stumble into the garage. A vampire is perched on top of my dad's SUV. Another one is circling the SUV slowly as my dad tracks it like a lion stalking its prey. My mom aims her crossbow at the one in front of my dad.

"It's my last stake," she says. "Make it count."

My dad grabs the vampire by its shoulders and they tussle at the side of the car. He tries to turn the vamp so it's facing my mom but the vamp is too strong. It slams my dad against the SUV and the window shatters behind his head. He wobbles on his feet and the vamp spins him around so that now my dad is between my mom and the vamp. She can't get a clear shot.

She grunts angrily. And then, from inside the SUV, through the shattered glass window, Cedrick's hand reaches out and in one quick motion he plants his stake in the vampire's back. The creature wails and in its confusion it lets my dad go. My mom lets loose her last stake and it hits the vamp, who disappears in a cloud of ash.

The vampire perched on the top of the SUV leaps toward me and just as it is about to crash into me, Aaron appears in a cloud of black smoke. He reaches out with his clawed fingers, sinking them into the other vampire's neck and pulling it down onto the floor of the garage. The vampire screams so loud I have to cover my ears. I stumble back and my mom shoves me against the wall.

"Traitor!" the vampire screams as it grapples with Aaron. "You betray your own kind!"

Aaron and the other vamp suddenly disappear in a charcoal-colored haze.

"Aaron!" I yell, but he's gone.

A moment later, something crashes through the roof of the garage, splintering the wood and sending debris flying everywhere. It lands on the hood of my dad's SUV. I'm afraid to look. I'm scared to death it's Aaron but when I get the nerve to look up, I realize it's the vampire he'd been fighting with. A stake protrudes from its chest as it disintegrates into a pile of ash.

"Get in the car!" Miss Celia yells from the other side of the garage.

The driver's-side door pops open and my mom lifts me off the ground by the straps of the bag I have slung across my back and tosses me inside. I scramble across the middle console and into the back seat where Jules and Cedrick are. 'Lita is lying across the third-row seats with her head in Miss Kim's lap. Mr. Rupert is passed smooth out and is slumped against the rear window.

"What's wrong with 'Lita?" I ask as panic grips me.

My mom dives into the car and my dad hops in the driver's seat and starts the engine.

"Celia!" my mom screams. "Get in here! Now!"

Miss Celia holds up her hand and at first I think there's a hole right in the middle of her palm but then I realize she's holding the Vanta-black orb. I follow her gaze and spot another vampire crawling its way through the hole in the roof of the garage.

"Cover your eyes!" I shout.

Miss Celia presses the button and light floods the garage. When I open my eyes there's a new cloud of smoke in the air and my mom is pulling Miss Celia through the open passenger's-side window.

Tires screech as my dad backs out of the garage. He doesn't even wait for the garage door to go up. We bust through the door and spin around in the driveway.

"My dads!" Cedrick screams as he reaches for the door handle. "We're not leaving without my dads!"

I peer through the back window and there's a flurry of movement in the garage. Mr. Ethan is suddenly standing in the center of the floor, his mask gone and his face stained with tears.

"Dad!" Cedrick yells. He pulls the handle and jumps out of the SUV before I can stop him.

"Cedrick, no!" my dad shouts.

Cedrick runs toward Mr. Ethan and then both Mr. Ethan and Cedrick are enveloped by a cloud of thick black mist.

"No!" I scream.

My mom is out of the car and 'Lita is pushing her way over the seat and out the door, too. She stands clutching her side, wincing with each breath. The cloud of mist pushes toward the SUV. My mom pauses, stumbles back, then climbs back inside the truck, slamming the door.

"'Lita!" Jules yells.

'Lita isn't even looking at the cloud as it moves closer to the truck. She's staring toward the gate at the end of our driveway.

"Lidia!" my mom shouts.

Suddenly, in a burst of frigid air, Cedrick is back inside the truck and next to him is Mr. Ethan. Aaron materializes outside and shoves 'Lita back toward the SUV, where Miss Celia grabs her and pulls her inside. Aaron's face appears outside the window.

"Go!" he shouts. "We'll keep them off you!"

We?

CHAPTER 13

My dad floors it and the truck lurches forward. Jules grabs hold of me. Cedrick clings to Mr. Ethan.

"Where's Dad?" Cedrick asks frantically. "Where is he?"

Mr. Ethan doesn't answer him. He has a vacant expression on his face.

"Where's Mr. Alex?" I ask through choked sobs.

The truck bounces over the curb as we barrel through the gate. Aaron appears in a cloud of mist outside the window and he is not alone. Mr. Alex is in the mist with him and at first I think Aaron's holding him, carrying him the same way he'd carried me, but no. Mr. Alex is too far away from Aaron in the cloud of inky mist.

"Mom," I say as the reality of what I'm watching hits me right in the chest. "Mom."

"I know," my mom says quietly. "I know."

My mind goes blank. I watch out the back window as we leave my house behind. The remaining vampires don't move from where they're positioned. I watch them get smaller and smaller as we drive away. My dad speeds out of the neighborhood and turns onto the highway.

We drive in silence as we follow the looping coils of highway. San Antonio is one of those places where you can drive for forty-five minutes and still be in the city. We're heading toward the east side of town and I rest my head in my hands as 'Lita cries in the seat next to me. She rubs my back and I hold Jules's hand. After a moment, I wrestle the duffel bag off my back and set it on the floor at my feet. The zipper is ripped and the stash of snacks I'd hidden inside have fallen out. The book from Cedrick's dads is open, some of the pages torn. I take it out and sit it in my lap. Feels silly to care about it at a time like this but the book was my responsibility and I promised Mr. Ethan and Mr. Alex I would take care of it.

I press the torn pages flat and try to adjust the binding, but it's cracked. I flip to the last page to see if maybe I can reattach everything with some clear tape when I get the chance, but something catches my eye in the shadowy confines of the truck. The binding is ripped, and the spine is disjoined. What I thought was the last page where my mom had written the last entry isn't really the last page after all. Tucked beneath the endpaper is another entry. A single sentence.

When you find this, know that you have only yourselves to blame.
Nat

My heart almost stops. Nat?

Suddenly, 'Lita's hands are slipping the book out of my lap and she's staring at the pages.

"'Lita," I whisper.

She gently pats my hand and sighs. "Tre," she says to my dad. "Take us to Mission Park."

"What?" my dad asks, confused. "No. Lidia, we don't have time. We need to get to the training facility and it's a three-hour drive."

"Training facility?" Jules asks.

I think it's weird, too, but what's even stranger is 'Lita's request. Mission Park is a cemetery and I don't understand why we need to go there.

"Tre," 'Lita repeats. "Trust me on this."

My dad glances at her in the rearview mirror and he nods.

Mission Park is forty-five minutes from my house and nobody says anything the entire ride except for Mr. Rupert, who wakes up and immediately starts complaining that we're going in the wrong direction. Everyone ignores him and eventually he just closes his mouth and sits back with his arms folded.

We arrive at Mission Park Cemetery and pile out of the

truck. 'Lita tucks the book with the strange entry under her arm, wincing and holding her side. She limps to the front gates of the sprawling cemetery without a word.

Aaron suddenly appears at my side and he takes my hand in his and squeezes it. I pull him close and hug him.

"I'm so glad you're okay," I say.

"Where's Mr. Alex?" my dad asks.

Aaron shakes his head. My heart sinks but suddenly Mr. Alex is right there, too. A cloud of gray smoke encircles him.

"Dad!" Cedrick squeals. He rushes toward him but stops short.

"Ceddy," Mr. Alex says. His voice gives it all away. The serum couldn't hold off the change.

Mr. Alex is a vampire now.

Miss Celia begins to sob. Mr. Rupert is, probably for the first time in his life, speechless. We all stare at Mr. Alex. Mr. Ethan is there immediately.

"You're still you," Mr. Ethan sobs.

Mr. Alex nods. "I know."

There is a long moment filled with tears and sobs and I don't know what to do. Tears cloud my eyes. I'm so angry that all of this is happening. That so many of the people I love are being hurt.

"What are we doing here?" I finally ask.

'Lita wipes the tears from her eyes as she enters the gates of the cemetery. "Come with me. I'm very worried that the tragedy of what has happened to Alex, to Aaron, may not be our biggest concern at this moment."

My parents look at each other.

"She's injured," my mom says. "It's not serious but maybe she's in a little bit of shock?"

My dad nods and we follow 'Lita as she cuts a path through the tombstones and mausoleums. She doesn't even look up. She knows exactly where she's going and when her final destination comes into view, I stop dead in my tracks.

In a quiet corner of the cemetery is the gravesite of Nightside. It's a small rectangular building made of black granite. It shimmers in the moonlight and the steps that lead to its front doors are littered with plastic stakes, wilted flowers, and all kinds of other little trinkets. People bring stuff to her grave to leave as a tribute. I'd been out here with 'Lita once but it was a long time ago.

'Lita marches up to the crypt and produces a large brass key from the pocket of her jacket. She fits it in the lock on the mausoleum door and it clicks open. She pushes through the door.

"Lidia," my dad says. "I know you're still mourning her but this is not the time. We have to get the kids to a safe spot. We have to make sure Alex is okay. We need to regroup."

'Lita turns and stands on the front step of the tomb. "I fought harder at the Reaping than I ever had in my entire life. I wanted to save us all."

My mom shakes her head. "Nobody did more for us that day than you. Come on, Lidia. Please come down from there."

"I didn't do enough," 'Lita says. She glances at Aaron and then at Mr. Alex, who is trailing Mr. Ethan and Cedrick. "I need your help."

"Mom," Miss Celia says, and it sounds strange hearing her say it. "Mom, please. You're injured. You're not thinking clearly."

"I have never been more clear in my life," 'Lita says. "And if I saw what I think I saw, we are in more danger than any of us can possibly imagine and from a foe who knows what our every move will be."

"What?" Miss Celia asks. "Who? You know who's behind all of this?"

"I didn't want to believe it," 'Lita says. "It should be impossible."

She touches the book, then gestures to Aaron and Mr. Alex and they join her just inside the mausoleum's doors. We all crowd the steps as 'Lita, Mr. Alex, and Aaron move inside and stand next to the narrow black box that sits in the center of the crypt. I've never seen this part of the gravesite before, only the outside. This box is where Nightside is buried.

"Aaron, Alex," 'Lita says. "Move the lid back."

Everyone looks at 'Lita like she has lost her entire mind.

"It's too heavy for me to move it alone," 'Lita says. "Please move it back for me."

Miss Kim steps forward and pulls Aaron back. "No. No way. What on earth for?"

Everyone starts talking at once. They're all telling 'Lita she's injured and isn't thinking straight and that she should sit down. She's shouting at them to listen to her.

"Lidia, this is uncalled for," Mr. Rupert says.

I slip the book from 'Lita's hands and flip to the hidden entry.

"When you find this, know that you have only yourselves to blame," I read aloud.

My mom's head snaps up and she eyes the book.

"What—what are you reading?" my mom asks.

"It's an entry I found under the endpaper," I say. "That's what it says and it's signed 'Nat.'"

No one speaks.

No one breathes.

"It is in her handwriting," 'Lita says.

My mom takes the book from me and looks it over. "No. There has to be an explanation."

'Lita shakes her head. "I saw her."

Silence swallows the inside of the crypt.

"Saw who?" my mom asks.

"Nightside," 'Lita says. "Natalia. Nat."

My mom steps toward 'Lita. "That's impossible. She's— she's dead."

'Lita stares at the granite black box that holds the mortal remains of Nightside. "Prove me wrong."

My mom looks at Mr. Alex and gives him a nod. Everyone takes a few steps back. Mr. Alex moves to the side of the coffin alongside Aaron and together they put their hands on the lid. With one quick shove, they push the lid back and it topples to the floor, breaking into pieces.

I hold my breath as the dust clears.

'Lita steps toward the coffin and peers inside, then turns to us.

"Empty."

ACKNOWLEDGMENTS

I'm so happy to be able to continue the story of Boog, Cedrick, Jules, Aaron, and the Vanquishers. This is a story about friendship, family, and of course . . . vampires! As I've said many times, I'm a vampire stan. From Anne Rice's vamps to Dracula, from *The Lost Boys* and *Blade* to *Twilight* (yes, *Twilight*), I love a good story about the undead and I'm having so much fun adding my take on these mythical creatures to the conversation.

I'd like to thank my agent, Jamie Vankirk, and my editor, Mary Kate Castellani, for helping me bring this story into the world. I'm grateful to the entire team at Bloomsbury for all the work they put into this book. Huge shoutout to Claudia Aguirre for another fabulous cover.

A big thank-you to my family and especially my kids, Amya, Elijah, Nye, and Lyla, for being my earliest readers and for sharing their thoughts and opinions about this story with me. I love y'all so much and I could not do this work without your love and support.

I'd like to thank the hundreds of students I've had the opportunity to visit, who loved the first book so much and who inspire me to keep the story going. I'd like to say hi to Winter, Carter, Cornelia, Ari, and Rosie. Look, y'all! You're in a book! You are all brilliant, capable, caring human beings who deserve everything good in this world. Keep being exactly who you are.

I don't get to be here writing these stories without the support of my readers, so I'd like to extend my sincerest gratitude to them. Thank you for sticking with me. I appreciate you more than you can possibly imagine.